HER SUNSET COWBOY

KATHY FAWCETT

CHAPTER 1

*F*ull dark came early to Wyoming in the fall.

Ridge West preferred to be home at his ranch before the sun went down. He knew late September roads in Wyoming could be treacherous after sunset, what with migrating wildlife crossing the road. And weather systems that blew in with no notice.

Lately, though, something in his gut had been pulling him to do idiotic things after dark.

Like this crazy mission he'd be ashamed to tell his sons, and terrified of disclosing to his daughters-in-law—climbing an old tree under a murky moon, with a sore knee and questionable night vision. The old maple made it easy, with branches close to the scrubby grass. Before he knew it, Ridge was four feet off the ground, feeling for the next place to put his hands.

"Hey, that's my leg!"

A woman's voice above him protested as he grabbed onto what he thought was a tree limb, but was one of *hers*.

"I thought it felt smoother than bark."

"Well I should hope so," she said, indignantly.

"Shh," Ridge cautioned, as he climbed up a few branches towards her. "Keep your voice down. We don't want anyone calling the police on us… again."

"Ridge West, get out of my *tree*," her now familiar voice commanded.

"It's not your tree," he said, infuriating her.

"Hurry up then," she half whispered. "I see a patrol car coming!"

Ridge groaned as his sore knee twinged in protest, but climbed another limb to where the beautiful Casey Parks was nestled in the crook of a branch. He found his own perch very near hers, while the headlights grew brighter.

As the two held their breath, officer Jason Scott, of the West Gorge Police Department, slowed his cruiser to a near stop in front of the abandoned house whose yard the tree stood in. Ridge and Casey froze.

You smell nice, Ridge thought but didn't say out loud. Or did he?

"Shh!" Casey shushed him in irritation, while trying not to smile. He wouldn't have seen it. There was only dim light coming from neighboring houses and one faraway street lamp. Thankfully, the maple had held its leaves to this point, but the next good wind and rain would wipe the branches bare.

When the police car finally moved on, Ridge and Casey exhaled in relief.

"I saw your car around the corner and figured you were here," he said. "Now tell me what you see."

"I see a wealthy rancher who has no business up a tree, at this house, or in my business, Ridge West. *I'm* the one in real estate. You have a very big and important ranch to run."

Ridge didn't answer. He allowed a blanket of silence to fall over them as they listened to the distant bugling of an elk, and the rustling of leaves as the wind picked up.

"One good gust and our cover is blown, Casey Parks," Ridge said at last. "Tell me the condition of the roof, which is why you're up here, and let's hightail it to our cars before the rain comes."

Casey sighed in defeat.

"Comps for the neighborhood are good, but the roof is sagging, as

I suspected. Probably insufficient rafters or undersized sheathing. My guess is, there's mold from the water getting in. Speaking of, it will be drizzling at the blind auction tomorrow so fewer bidders—but the house is a dicey purchase," Casey summed up. "I'll probably pass."

Ridge smiled a slightly wicked grin.

"Glad to hear it, I already bought it."

Casey opened her mouth in shock.

"You... what? How?"

"Wish I'd known about the roof, though. I probably paid too much."

Casey silently seethed before responding.

"Then *what*... are you doing up here?"

"To tell you not to bother showing up at the auction. There won't be one," he said, "now let's get out of my tree."

Insufferable man, Casey thought to herself. If she were a cartoon character, there would be steam coming out of her ears right about now.

"You could have sent me a text!"

"Then I couldn't help you down."

Ridge put his foot on a lower branch and started the careful process of extricating himself from the maple, guiding Casey as he went. "Put your foot here... now here."

"Get away from me, Ridge," she kicked her foot at him in protest. "I can do this myself."

"Nonsense," he said. "Getting up and down are different animals. You could get hurt."

If only he knew, Casey thought.

The great and mighty Ridge West had no idea how very hurt and down she had been—both personally and professionally. Which is why she was hiding out in West Gorge in the first place. She had taken the ultimate tumble off a high branch. But by the grace of God, had managed to blend in and even rebuild some in the past few years.

But Ridge threatened to ruin everything.

She couldn't seem to buy a house or climb a tree without bumping into him. He was in her business—*literally*. Most days, Casey wanted

3

to strangle him. Other days, she wondered what it would be like to kiss him. But no matter how piercing his eyes were when they looked at her, or how much her hands wanted to touch his thick silvery hair, she didn't dare let him get close.

If he knew who she was, he'd run for the hills and she'd be humiliated all over again. She couldn't bear the thought of making a fresh start in yet another town. But how much longer could she stand his shadowing and taunting?

Ridge made it down first and stood on the ground, offering his hand. Ignoring him, she jammed her foot onto each limb in anger. On the lowest branch, while thinking words a lady didn't say, Casey shoved her shoe into the crook and felt it stick in the rough bark—it wouldn't budge. But she had momentum, and the rest of her body was going down with or without her foot.

She shouted out in a panic.

"Ridge!"

Suddenly, his one offered hand became two arms trying to break her fall.

Casey landed on top of Ridge with a loud and ungainly *oof* as they fell to the ground. Ridge expelled a loud *oof* of his own as the wind was sucker punched out of his lungs.

Groaning and clumsy in the dark, they clutched onto each other, rolling this way and that before finally separating and settling on their backs—Ridge holding his sore knee, and Casey her ankle.

"Are you okay?" Ridge was the first to catch his breath.

"I twisted my foot," Casey managed, looking straight up at the stars and breathing hard. "I think I'll sue the homeowner... oh wait, that's *you.*"

Ridge managed a single laugh, but it sounded more like a pained cough.

"You didn't want this rickety old house..." he panted, "anyway."

"You didn't know that," she said, exhaling heavily. "I think you only bought it because you thought I did want it. Well joke's on you."

They were silent for a minute, both rallying their energy for the next round.

"And I think that *you* think pretty highly of yourself," Ridge drawled, with a smirk in his voice that stirred up Casey's anger all over again. "I'm not sitting around thinking of you. I'm thinking of the town, and getting this eye-sore turned around."

Casey was quiet still.

"As you pointed out, it's going to take a pretty penny to fix up this bucket of rust," Ridge went on, "I was saving you, or another buyer, from getting in over your head. That's all."

"As for my part," Casey said, unable to remain silent, "thanks but no thanks. I don't need you to protect me or rescue me, Ridge West. Not from maple trees or ramshackle houses. I only need you to stay away!"

When he didn't answer, Casey pressed him. Her frustration evident in her voice as she sounded near tears. "Do you think you can handle that?"

Before either could say another word, the first raindrops of the night fell and hit them squarely on their faces as they gazed up at the cloudy sky.

"Sure," Ridge said with a pained grimace on his face, thinking that getting in Casey's business had brought him nothing but misery and discomfort, and he really was too old for either. But it had also been a tiny bit of fun—though one sided, apparently.

And while he would try to honor her wishes, about trees at least, he couldn't leave her lying in the rain on a dark cold night. Standing with some effort and a few loud groans, Ridge reached his hand out to help Casey stand up.

"One last rescue," he said.

CHAPTER 2

"*I*s it my imagination, or is that knee getting *worse?*"

Ridge didn't expect to find the boys in the kitchen the following morning—the boys being his oldest son, and the family's bachelor cousins from the north. He thought he could fly under the radar, and limp to get his coffee in privacy. But Gunnar was finishing his breakfast along with cousins Rowdy and Gray, who had become permanent fixtures on the ranch.

After selling their own West Ranch in Montana, these two gladly relocated to Wyoming to help Gunnar, with Colton and Pike leaving for other ventures.

Rowdy West was a retired rodeo rider who had missed the day-to-day operations of ranch living. Gray West was a rancher, and also a pilot who volunteered to extinguish wildfires in the mountains. The two had taken over the guest house with everyone's full blessing.

Ridge knew they started work before first light, and often came in for a mid-morning meal. Ridge suspected Gunnar wanted to play with baby Willow, now awake. The toys strewn along the tile floor of the massive ranch kitchen confirmed his suspicions.

As Ridge poured his coffee and stepped over squeaky toys, Gunnar asked him again.

"You're really limping, Dad. What gives?"

"Hmmm," Ridge mumbled, trying to deflect the situation, but all eyes were on him. The last thing he needed was for doctor Kat to walk in and join the chorus. He'd either have to come clean about climbing a tree—which had been fine until a certain someone fell on him like a sack of feed corn, or fabricate an answer.

He didn't want to do either.

"Don't you have a ranch to run?" Ridge bristled to the grown men, all towering around him like oak trees, even in their socks.

Socks.

Ridge and his sons had been coming in and out of the big house for years in their boots. Always moving fast as they cared for the growing ranch, they never had time for such *civilities* as wearing house slippers. But once Kat gave birth to little Willow, and started gaining confidence within the big house, she laid down the law.

"We've got a crawler," she told the cowboys. "I'll not have her dredging her sweet self through the dirt, dust, and sagebrush that y'all track in on your boots. And I certainly don't have time to sweep every minute."

Which was true. As head of the Infectious Disease Department at the West Gorge hospital, Kat was busy. She also spent part of her time running the charitable foundation that Ridge's wife started years ago. When Randi died, the West Foundation lost its leader—until Kat stepped in.

Ridge was grateful for Kat West and gave her full reign. He knew someone needed to take ownership of the enormous home and that, left to their own devices, the men would reduce the beautiful marble, oak and steel within the walls to a rustic bunkhouse.

They had proven that.

"All right, we can talk later," Gunnar said to Ridge with a smile. "The hands are tallying hay bales for winter over in the north section, if you're at all interested in ranch life today."

Ridge wondered if that was a subtle dig at his new interest in real estate.

For many years, he too had been up before the sun, happily

heading out for the day with the cowboys. And for a few years after Randi died, he went through the motions. But little by little, Gunnar took the lead at West Ranch, with Colton and Pike's help. And bit by bit, Ridge pulled back.

He was never sure who was the chicken and who was the egg in this scenario, but the result was the same. Nobody expected him to come out anymore.

"Oh," Gunnar stopped and turned around again, "I got word Chuck Barber's ranch is finally going on the market. Thought you might be interested."

"Odd time of year," Ridge said, knowing ranches usually came on the market in early spring, not at the onset of winter. "It'll be buried in snow before long."

"I thought the same," Gunnar said, "but Chuck's sons never were too sharp."

Ridge waved the men off, and settled in with his coffee and daily newspaper. After a time, he refilled his mug and padded in his slippers through the kitchen and into the large foyer. Weak sunlight came through the cut glass windows of the double oak and iron doors, which led to a covered portico where visitors could drive up and avoid Wyoming downpours or blizzards.

Inside, Kat contracted a fancy new marble floor, with a patterned inlay of glossy wood and geode crystals.

The overall effect in the foyer was stunning and elegant.

She kept the antler chandelier, to Ridge's relief. It was one of his wife's favorite pieces. But Kat added recessed spotlights, trained on a new display of family photos—beautiful wedding portraits of Gunnar and Kat, Pike and Paislee, and most recently, Colton and Liu. There was an adoption photo of Ash, and a baby portrait of Willow, among others.

Soon, there would be a graduation portrait as Ash finished high school, and probably more babies, which suited Ridge just fine.

At the center of the display hung the center of the family—Randi Lynn West, as painted by Pike West. Their son managed to capture her kindness and intelligence, as well as her long golden hair and fiery spirit.

She was a young attorney from Michigan when she first arrived in West Gorge, bearing the countenance of a Nordic goddess. She conducted her business of purchasing West land for the Ford Motor Company and never left. Randi fell into Ridge's arms and into his wild Wyoming life as if born to it.

"Ah, but you're gone now, lass," Ridge said to the painting, reaching up to touch her, only to find flat, cold canvas under his fingertips.

He could see that his hands looked older and more weathered, while Randi stayed frozen in time through the painting. In the mirror, the tanned lines around his eyes were more pronounced. His hair was nearly silver, from the brownish-blonde he used to be.

Dishwater, Randi had sweetly called his hair color, as her slender fingers would eagerly become tangled in his thick curls, pulling his lips towards her own.

"The only dishwater you'll ever know, cowboy," she lovingly joked.

As Ridge walked into the great room and over by the crackling fire, he used his free hand to hold onto the backs of chairs, babying his knee. But the twinges were no big deal—he'd gotten used to walking with pain.

It was this other sensation that took him by surprise: anticipation.

Lately, Ridge had been opening his eyes each morning with a new eagerness that he couldn't quite put his finger on. All he was doing was buying and flipping houses—what possible magic could come out of that?

CHAPTER 3

"*SOLD* to Casey Parks."

The auctioneer shouted Casey's four favorite words as the assembled group grumbled and disbanded. She smiled in private triumph—nobody stole the sale at the last minute. But looking around, there was nobody to congratulate her, either. In the old days, her father would be with her, or one of their several employees.

Amber, her part-time intern, was around somewhere, probably perusing the contents of the house, spread out on folding tables in the garage and along the driveway. The high-school senior worked with Casey for extra credit and, it seemed, an inside track on vintage clothing and jewelry.

Not even out of school, Amber had a profitable online store, named *Amber Waves*.

Casey smiled—she was alone, but this was a good day. With a little work, the house would be a lucrative rental for families coming to West Gorge for a Wyoming vacation. Bigger than the small bungalows she scooped up when she could afford to, the tri-level would accommodate three or four couples for a ski trip. Or a larger family avoiding pricey hotels, who preferred to cook their own meals.

Maybe Amber could keep her eye out for a set of vintage dishes for this kitchen, Casey thought. She had stock plates in bulk for her other rentals, but today she was feeling domestic. And nostalgic. This retro house, with its cantilevered roofline and sunken family room, reminded Casey of her happy childhood in Arizona with her parents.

The auctioneer jokingly called it the *Brady Bunch* house, but it wouldn't be for long.

She would dress two bedrooms with log bunk beds, and swap the shag carpet for engineered wood. With a little work, it could be listed for the upcoming ski season. Like her gramma used to say to lazy kids and plump chickens, "it's time to earn your keep."

Looking up at the mountains, Casey took a deep breath of the chilled autumn air and smiled with satisfaction. She had a rush of adrenaline from the victory, and it made her hungry. She would take Amber to celebrate at the diner over omelets and toast. Unless her intern had to get back for afternoon classes, that is.

This thought made Casey feel just a little pathetic, knowing her only friend in town had a curfew and a babysitting job on the side.

"You really need to meet people your own age," Amber told her recently.

"How?" Casey truly wanted to know.

"Well, there was a town picnic last month at Rotary Park," Amber said, "you should have gone. Or you could join the church choir. I hear they're looking for altos to balance out Bud Shire's wife on Handel's *Messiah*. My mom says her soprano is… enthusiastic."

"Hmm," Casey frowned, unconvinced.

West Gorge was a small town with the same familiar faces. But she had been devoted solely to her work since arriving a few years back, determined to start over with the little seed money she had. There wasn't time for chatty civic groups—she had to be her own charity in order to survive her shameful exit from Phoenix. No time for church, BBQ socials, or singing with the choir—Sundays were for open houses, or painting drab walls to entice renters and buyers.

Rebuilding a life from the ground up was a thankless and lonely job.

Pushing a few curls off her face that wouldn't stay tucked behind her ear, Casey pulled her collar higher against the chill morning breeze, then stuffed her hands in her pockets only to discover an unexpected warmth.

Gloves!

Happily, she'd gotten into the habit of storing her flannel-lined coats fully stocked every year, and ready for anything.

After some resistance, Casey had to admit the laid-back Wyoming work attire of jeans, boots, and plaid shirts suited her more than the severe power suits she'd worn in Phoenix. She felt different and nicer, and *younger* in flannel.

She tailored the soft shirts though, in the wee hours of the night while watching old movies and the home renovation channel. Maybe someday she'd let the hems hang like shapeless boxes on her hips, but today wasn't that day.

Smiling to herself, Casey recalled her early days in West Gorge, wearing expensive linen and wool suits while out on the dusty streets of the ranching town. In her interview, Amber had been the first brave enough to tell her the truth.

"Some think you're a big-city lawyer, or undertaker," she said. "Folks have a bet going."

One man, whose log house listing Casey desperately wanted under contract, slammed his door on what he was sure was an IRS agent. "Taxes are in the mail," he shouted.

Now she blended in, looking more like a local than *trouble* from out of town.

Flannel and jeans were great equalizers for everybody in Wyoming, making it hard to tell whether a man was a cowboy or a millionaire. Or both, like the man gazing at her from across the yard. As the sea of bidders parted in defeat, Casey saw *him* leaning against a tree in the front yard, wearing a half smile that didn't quite reach his smoldering eyes. It was Ridge, of course.

Casey sucked in a sharp breath at seeing him, but otherwise stood as still as a sculpted marble statue as he appraised her from under the brim of his cowboy hat. She hadn't seen him in a few days—since they tumbled out of a tree and then ran, or hobbled rather, in the rain to their cars.

She could still feel the warmth of his hand as he gently tugged her along.

We're nearly there, he had shouted through sheets of water pouring down. And though her ankle stung and they were soaked to the bone, she wished she'd parked farther away that night.

Now, her stomach and nerves tumbled together under his gaze. Standing as straight and tall as her curves would allow, Casey was glad he couldn't see the adrenaline shooting through her. Though the blush on her cheeks probably gave her away.

Go ahead and look, she thought. *See what else you'll never have, besides this house.*

CHAPTER 4

"*A*nother *Parks Place* feather in your cap."

Ridge sidled his way up to congratulate her—one strong cowboy leg at a time. Biting the inside of her lip, Casey tried to take her eyes off his legs; the legs that climbed ladders like a teenager, and rescued real estate agents stuck in trees.

"Or a big lemon if no one rents it." Casey shrugged and tried to sound self-deprecating, which seemed to amuse Ridge.

He tilted his head and smiled as he searched her face.

"Nah," he concluded with a slight shake of his head. "You don't make rookie purchases. This tri-level is money, and I think you know that."

Casey's mouth felt dry at his nearness and unexpected compliment. She was at a complete loss as to what to say next, so instead, worked to slow her breathing just enough to pull off a smile.

Real estate sales in this town had been as exciting as oatmeal before Ridge West started to show an interest. Why he did, she wasn't sure. These little homes must be small potatoes to a man who owned half the town, and one of the biggest ranches in the state.

It seemed to Casey that his obsession started when he lost the little Madison house to her, the one next door to his son, Ash. If she could walk it backwards, she would let him buy it instead—like tossing an offering of snow-white orchids into a volcano to keep it from erupting. Because buying that one little house opened up a can of real estate warfare between the two, and she couldn't put the lid back on.

That didn't seem right, though. Ridge was a grown man. He should be used to a little friendly competition in business. Now, everything she wanted, he seemed to want too.

Sometimes it added a thrill to the chase—but only when she won. Sure, it made the victories sweeter, but it also made the defeats more bitter than they ought to be.

Ridge's strategy, as far as Casey could tell, was to shadow her, and out-bid her when the spirit moved him. Even beyond market value. Sometimes he didn't bid at all—just stood nearby and made her jumpy, wondering whether he was going to snatch the house at the last minute.

She ought to hate him for it, but she didn't. It was kind of fun, in a way real estate hadn't been fun for her in years.

And today, she bested him.

The auction house moved up the sale date for the tri-level, and Casey doubted everyone got the memo. Especially not a dinosaur like Ridge West, who wasn't hooked up to his phone like an I.V.

And no, she didn't feel guilty for not telling him. If he insisted on dipping his boots in her living, she'd find every way possible to stay ahead of his deep pockets.

"It's going to take some elbow grease, though," Ridge said, nodding at the house skeptically, bringing her back to the present.

"These sixties structures have good bones," Casey answered, "and a lot of life in them."

"Hmm. I sure hope that's true," he drawled with a slow burn of a smile that Casey felt as much as saw as it travelled through her, warming some icy bits of self-preservation.

She just knew he was talking about himself and not the house, and tried not to gaze at his tanned hand resting on his abs. The abs weren't quite washboard, she didn't think, but judging by the smooth tuck of his shirttail into his jeans, they could hold their own.

Yes, good bones.

"Wish I'd known about the new auction date, though." His smile faded just a bit.

"Shame," she said, not sounding at all sincere.

"Yes, a pity."

"You know Ridge, there's a lot of pivoting in the real estate market."

"*Pivoting,* that's a new one."

"Agents these days have to be nimble."

"Nimble, huh?"

"Maybe *nimble* just it isn't your thing." Casey saw his expression fall as she spoke.

"Maybe you're right," he shrugged as a shadow of self-doubt crossed his face.

Almost immediately, guilt washed over Casey at her comment. Ridge West was a strong, robust man. Who was she to take the wind out of his sails? Opening her mouth to apologize, her guilt turned to shock at his next words.

"Or, maybe while you were here, I was busy buying that pretty blue colonial over on Jasper," he told her.

"No, you couldn't have!" Casey objected quickly, knowing full well the colonial was under contract with an auction house. "That sale is slated for next week."

Ridge smiled again. This time, his mirth reached his eyes in mischievous sparks, and fine handsome crinkles that she was drawn to in spite of her anger.

Standing to his full height, he leaned forward with his lips slightly parted. For a crazy moment, Casey thought he was going to kiss her and her heart raced... then he spoke in a husky whisper, "maybe *nimble* is my thing, after all."

His warm breath made her shiver.

"Ma'am," he said.

Touching the brim of his hat, Ridge turned to take his leave.

CHAPTER 5

"*D*ang, it's getting hot in here."

Amber held a box filled with treasures as she walked up to a seething Casey.

"What do you mean *hot...* we're outside in the cold," Casey responded in confusion.

"You and Ridge West, steaming up this auction like a couple of lava rocks in a sauna," Amber said. "You got the house, right?"

Casey shook her head to clear her thoughts.

"Yes... this one, anyway."

Ridge just couldn't let her have her moment without pulling the rug out from under her, could he? Casey kicked herself for letting him one-up her today. It was becoming routine.

He was a distraction—a magnificent distraction. The way he touched his hat and whispered that he'd stolen yet another house made her heart pound at his... *audacity*. He came so close to her, then tipped his hat and left.

Ma'am.

Mad as she was, she couldn't take her eyes off of the angles and muscles and *power* of Ridge as he turned and walked away.

"I'll get him next time," she told Amber distractedly.

17

Her intern, wearing a West Gorge Seniors sweatshirt, rolled her eyes and told Casey she was going back to the office.

"See you there," Amber said, without waiting. Her boss was a million miles away.

Uh huh, she would get him next time, Casey thought, waving distractedly to Amber. She felt deflated, in spite of winning the bid on the house.

Coming to West Gorge hadn't been easy. She had to overcome the good ol' boys' network through late hours and diligence. She tirelessly mined scraps of information on every property, like this tri-level. But Ridge, increasingly a step ahead, was knocking her off her game. Even now, when she should be focused on work instead of how handsome he looked.

It was amazing though, how a woman's tastes could change through the years—she wouldn't have given him a second glance in her twenties or thirties. But somewhere in her late forties, the silvery stubble on a man's tanned jawline became very attractive.

"More salt than pepper," Casey said under her breath as she watched Ridge from a distance, and admired his soft bristles. At least, she imagined they were soft.

After his rugged good looks, it was his voice that rattled her. That gravelly sound of Ridge West saying her name, even in anger. When he talked, she could *feel* as much as hear that low rumble stir up her insides, like so many rocks in a tumbler.

Easy girl, Casey cautioned herself.

But how could she resist the guilty pleasure of watching him walk away? Ridge West was a rancher and a cowboy. An athlete who hadn't lost an ounce of muscle with time.

Oh, there was that slight limp, which he still blamed her for. But that made him all the more appealing. She smiled at the memory of Ridge tumbling off a ladder trying to peek at a pre-auction home. It was late at night, and she snuck into that same house with her flashlight. Shining the beam on Ridge in the window, her scream startled him into falling.

It was almost funny, but for his injury—and the nosey neighbor who called the police.

Casey felt bad about the incident, but wouldn't let him know. They were both in the wrong place, and acting like adolescents. Spending a few hours in the town jail cell with Ridge may not be one of his fondest memories, but it was one of hers.

Now, because of Ridge's youngest son Ash, they had become unlikely colleagues. *Frenemies,* as Amber would say. Ash owned the bungalow he inherited from his grandmother, and Ridge and Casey owned the little homes on each side.

Three bears, Ridge named the houses—and Casey thought it was apt. There was Papa bear and baby bear, but no mama bear; she liked to think of herself as the ambitious real estate bear who kept her enemies close.

"Let's work together on the renovations, and save money where we can," Casey suggested to the West men. Ash eagerly agreed and Ridge went along for his son's sake.

Ash was a good kid; he was hungry and eager to learn the business from her. He wasn't raised with privilege, like the other Wests. And there was pain in him, not so deep down. Not a visible pain like Ridge's limp, but pain she saw in his eyes.

Pulling herself back to the present, Casey made her way to the auctioneer's table to sign the necessary paperwork. She saw Ridge walking to his truck after breaking away from a group of men.

Instinctively, her body lurched a little towards him.

Whoa, girl.

It was an old cowboy trick. A wild horse will follow someone who turns and walks away, she knew. And some days she was tempted to just follow Ridge West, wherever he was going. Slink up behind him and slip her hand into the back pocket of his soft-as-river-water blue jeans. Something she hadn't done since she was Amber's age.

But she couldn't. Not today or ever.

The last time she thought a man was cute walking away, he was walking away with everything she'd ever worked for. Leaving her with no choice but to run, and hide out in sleepy little West Gorge, Wyoming.

CHAPTER 6

imble!

Ridge practically spat the word into the dry dirt next to his truck at the tri-level auction before getting in and driving off. He never should have come. He showed up for one reason, and that was to gloat a little—only, it wasn't a clean kill.

He wanted to see Casey Parks' shocked face when he told her he bought the colonial. The reaction was there, but he didn't feel good about it. Anger flashed on her face, but then she looked lonely and sad. *Beautiful* and lonely and sad. Making his expensive gesture look small and mean.

He sure didn't need another house, or to collect them like toys. He really only ever wanted the one—the Madison bungalow, next door to the little house his son Ash inherited from his grandmother. The house he was peeking at when he fell off the ladder.

But Casey Parks won that round. She had her assistant buy it as her proxy while they were stuck in jail, and both his pride and leg took a beating. Only one could be helped by physical therapy though. The other, he'd have to work through on his own.

He opened up to her that night, and told her that all he wanted was to stay close to Ash while the boy renovated his granny's house.

Maybe he was too used to getting his way, but he thought that sentimental disclosure would be enough.

It wasn't.

In time, though, Miss Emily, the elderly friend and neighbor from the other side of Ash's house, offered to sell to him before she moved. Now, they were three bungalows in a row—the *three bears*. There was Ash, her royal highness, and himself, the *odd bear out*. Always landing in the dog house over something, these days.

"Way to go, Dad," Ash scolded him recently, "you're single-handedly inflating housing prices in West Gorge by spending more than the market will support. Now sellers expect too much money, and *real* buyers have to pay more than the houses are worth."

Real buyers! Huh.

His adopted son just finished his AP summer business class before his senior year of high school, and was flush with book knowledge. Ridge grumbled his response to Ash. "They won't teach you this in school, but anything is worth what someone is willing to pay for it."

However, not so deep down, he knew the boy was right and was a little ashamed at going too far. But the pull of seeing Casey Parks flash fireworks from her beautiful eyes when he drove up a sales price was strong.

She was a beautiful woman and he was drawn to her like... well, like he'd only been drawn to one other, and that was Randi Lynn. His wife and life partner succumbed to cancer five long years ago, and he missed her.

Ridge would never love again, he knew that much.

He didn't even *like* Casey. He wasn't sure what it was he felt. Only, he was feeling something, and it was a refreshing change from heartache. He tried to be amiable when he could—going along with Casey's plans for renovating their three homes as a group.

"Economy of scale," she said.

"Buying in bulk," Ridge said.

He wasn't concerned about the renovation costs but knew Casey and Ash were. And he was a good businessman, excited about a new venture. But somehow, he let it become an unhealthy competition, making everyone around him unhappy.

Gunnar wished he was working at the ranch.

Ash expected him to help more with the bungalow renovations.

Kat wanted him to focus on his health, and take care of his knee.

And Casey, Ridge suspected, wished him as far away from her as humanly possible.

CHAPTER 7

*P*aislee West had been at the ranch having lunch with Kat and baby Willow, who was showing off by pulling herself up to stand, and threatening to take her first steps.

After the baby went down for a nap, Paislee told Kat about her September trip to Denver with Pike. They left right after Colton's wedding to Liu Chen, the new ranch chef, and spent a few weeks with her parents, Pepper and Drake Andrews, and Paislee's two sisters.

"Our first wedding anniversary already," Paislee said.

"And our second," her sister-in-law said with a smile. "September is a big month for the West clan. How is your family?"

Paislee filled Kat in on the very wealthy Andrews' and their historic Denver home. Her spirited grandmother, Gigi, had moved in with the family, much to Paislee's relief. Gigi was keeping Paislee's parents on their toes.

"She wants steak for dinner, and won't eat her vegetables. Gigi spends hours on the computer day-trading. Mama says it's like having a teenaged boy in the house."

The older of Paislee's two sisters worked at the family bank, FSB, and earned a big promotion, which Paislee and Pike went to help celebrate. The way her sister was going, she would inherit FSB when Drake was ready to retire.

Paislee's father seemed more relaxed to now have an heir *and* a son-in-law.

For a time, he had been pushing an unsavory fellow on Paislee just to have someone to trust with the bank. But the man had turned out to be not so nice, and thankfully was found out in time. Paislee heard he was doing well at the Hong Kong office and wished him well, sort of.

These days, Paislee didn't waste much time thinking about anyone but her husband, Pike West. The sweet cowboy who rescued her from a snow storm, from a bad guy, and from a life that was going in the wrong direction. Now, she was happier than she ever thought possible.

Their new modern farmhouse in West Gorge was absolutely beautiful and she delighted in decorating and procuring art for their blank walls. Pike was doing his share; since leaving West Ranch, he'd been busy in his painting studio. But he enjoyed seeing other artists' work on his walls, and fully supported Paislee's expeditions.

She thought that would make her happy, but what she really wanted now was a baby in her arms. They were still newlyweds, but she loved Pike so much, and loved her life. She wanted to share all that love with children.

On the day they moved into the house, Pike joked about someday having 10 kids running around. They laughed, but certainly had the room. And when Paislee looked out her back door, she knew exactly where she wanted a playhouse and swing set. She would talk to Colton about that.

Thinking of Colton and Liu, Paislee said goodbye to Kat and Willow, and decided to drive over and say hello before heading home. Everyone had given the newlyweds space since their ceremony three weeks ago, but surely Colton was at work. She wouldn't stay long.

Walking up to the cook house, Paislee was certain she heard a baby crying, but Willow was with Kat. Liu opened the door before Paislee could even knock and sure enough, she held a tiny pink bundle in her arms, squirming and howling.

The ranch cook's normally pristine kitchen was a chaotic explosion of partially chopped and half prepared foods, mingled with baby formula and a sink filled with bottles.

Down the hall, through the open door of the laundry room, Paislee could spot an overflowing hamper of little blankets, and a drying rack with sleepers thrown over the assorted spindles.

The cook house, recently renovated and normally fabulous, was a mess.

Liu looked miserable and red-faced, and was about to cry along with the baby she was bouncing, trying to calm her.

"Wow, a baby. You and Colton work fast," Paislee joked.

Liu tried to smile but was obviously too frazzled. "Here, I've had to pee for two hours," she said, handing the baby to Paislee and dashing off.

Paislee took the little one in her arms and started cooing and rocking her gently.

Hush little baby, don't you cry, she sang.

She was at least half Chinese, maybe three months old, with the most beautiful round face. Paislee started kissing her cheeks and the baby quieted and relaxed in her arms. As she tipped her head and sang, Paislee's long hair fell off her shoulders in silky waves that tented the baby in darkness and safety.

There we go, that's it, she crooned.

By the time Liu returned, the exhausted infant was asleep on her shoulder. Paislee slowly moved to one of the stools at Liu's island and sat down, continuing to pat the baby gently on her back.

"Now," she whispered to Liu, who was making tea, "who is this angel?"

CHAPTER 8

"This is Sun," Liu said. "It's spelled s-u-n, but pronounced *soon* —as in, her birth mother went back to China, and isn't returning anytime soon! If ever."

"Oh no," Paislee exclaimed, squeezing the baby tighter. "And her daddy?"

Liu merely shrugged, while Paislee shook her head in true sadness.

Over tea, Liu went on to tell Paislee how the abandoned baby ended up in the care of her elderly great grandmother who lives alone in Rock Springs near Liu's family, the Chens. The grandma isn't well, and became overwhelmed. Ling Chen, Liu's mother, asked if she and Colton would take her in for a spell.

"I think they're hoping we'll adopt her."

Liu looked like she wanted to cry. Paislee reached over and took Liu's hand.

"Is that what you want?"

"I'm not sure," Liu said simply. "I just got married. I want to be a mother someday. Just not *today*. Did I mention we just got married? We have our honeymoon coming up, and... is it selfish to want time with Colton?"

"You are a newlywed, Liu," Paislee said. "You should *not* be crying like this."

"But she's so tiny and helpless. And her mother is Chinese, and I'm Chinese…" Liu said, shaking her head in frustration.

"All of those things are true," Paislee said. "Let me take her home for the afternoon and spell you. I have a crib for Willow's visits, and some of her infant clothes at the house."

"You'd do that?" Liu said, sounding hopeful.

"If your family won't mind," Paislee said.

"They would be grateful, I'm sure," Liu said. "My mother knows I'm in over my head."

Paislee gave the sleeping baby a joyful squeeze, and couldn't help but smile at the thought of caring for the little bundle for a few hours.

"We're going to have so much fun, aren't we Sun?"

Liu smiled and shook her head in wonder.

"I haven't been able to get her to sleep, Paislee," Liu said. "You're a natural."

Later, when Colton came home from the subdivision that his company, West Development, was building in town, Liu met him at the door and fell into his arms. Holding her tight, he looked around the house. It wasn't quite as destroyed as when he'd left that morning, feeling quite guilty for abandoning Liu with the unsettled newborn.

And it was *quiet.*

"Is she finally sleeping?" He pulled away and looked at her face. He couldn't quite tell if Liu was happy or not—he'd only been a husband for a few weeks, and still had a lot to learn.

"She's gone for the day. With Auntie Paislee," Liu said, and then sobbed. "I feel so relieved. And so guilty. And then I feel *guilty* to feel relieved!"

Colton pulled her close again.

Yep, he thought. *He had a lot to learn.*

CHAPTER 9

"*Y*ou again?"

Patricia's loud voice carried over the cold marble floors of the old West Gorge courthouse with an echo. Ridge cringed as he looked around to see who else might be listening, but they were alone, except for two or three others filing papers in the back.

When the new county buildings went up a dozen years ago, the old courthouse became home of the Land and Deed office, where Ridge's childhood friend Patricia ran a tight ship. And she was right—since he'd started buying real estate in West Gorge, he couldn't escape the high-volume run-ins with her.

"I've seen more of you these past months than when we were in school," she said.

"Patricia," Ridge greeted her warmly, but warily. "How's Hank?"

"Same as the last time you asked," she boomed, "three days ago."

Ridge knew his land holdings were already the stuff of legend, and yet in buying a few homes in the town, he felt like he was striking out on his own and making something that had his name alone on it. Unlike everything his ancestors handed to him—to all the Wests.

His great grandmother Addie came down from Montana in the

1800s to buy land and start a new life. Together with her husband, Pickford West, they tamed and ranched and established the town. Working together, the two bought up as many acres as they could stand to homestead. Then passed the land down to Ridge and his family—Ash, his eldest Gunnar, then Pike and Colton.

His granddaughter Willow marked a new generation of Wests.

Except for Ash, everyone was married, and busy with their lives. Too busy for Ridge. Not that he wanted much from them. He wanted his own thing; something different and new, like real estate.

It felt good to buy property and win auctions, then see his name on the deeds. But that Casey Parks, she made it personal. She hated to see him buy anything she might want for herself, and couldn't hide the fireworks when she was mad. If he was honest, he'd admit that he provoked her every now and then, just to have a front row seat. But West Gorge was no longer a one-horse town. There were enough properties to go around, in Ridge's view.

Patricia didn't support what he was doing, and said so. She and everybody else seemed fixated on the fact that just maybe he owned enough of West Gorge and didn't need to compete with the realtors, but he thought that was none of their business.

Wisely, he kept his opinions to himself, which is more than he could say about Patricia. He couldn't avoid her though, and had to file his newest acquisition with the county.

"If you ask me, what you're doing is just greedy," she told him.

Patricia always got away with saying whatever was on her mind.

"I didn't ask you," he said. "Real estate is just a side hustle—everyone has one."

She laughed her familiar wicked laugh, the one that made him want to run for cover.

"People here have side hustles so they can afford to heat their homes through the long winter, Ridge, you know that. Not because they're bored in their *castles*, or restless."

"I don't live in a…"

Was he bored and restless?

"Anyway Patricia, here's the application for the deed to the house on Jasper." Ridge slapped the paperwork down hard on the counter. "I bought it fair and square."

"Fair and square, huh? Why, your tactics and antics are the talk of the town," she laughed once more, then grew serious as she shook her head in wonder. "I never thought I'd see the day when Ridge West would become the town bad boy."

"Is that what you think of me?"

"Doesn't matter what I think."

"Sure it does."

Patricia looked at Ridge. She'd known him her entire life. He was a good man who had every right to lose his way a time or two. He'd had a mighty big love, and therefore a tremendous loss. She knew there were a lot of things warring inside of him at the prospect of moving on with his life.

"Ridge, do you remember when we were kids in middle school, and the gym teacher had to sit you boys down, and tell you all that when you liked a girl, poking her in the arm was the wrong way to show her?"

"I'm not sure I remember that," Ridge fibbed. He remembered it well.

"I don't believe you," Patricia said.

Her voice softened as she caught and held Ridge's eye. "If you like the girl… stop poking her in the arm, Ridge West."

WALKING TO HIS TRUCK, Ridge hung his head.

A man could do worse than having a friend like Patricia who had the guts to tell him the truth. He had been poking Casey in the arm, for sure. But *did* he like the girl? If he did, that was news to him. There were pretty women in town, he figured she was just one more.

But then, Casey was the only real estate agent he ever wanted to rescue from a tree, or stand behind at an auction. She sure made looking at paint chips at the hardware store more fun than it ought to be.

At least he didn't steal that tri-level from Casey. Ridge knew she wanted it badly. And of course he knew the date had changed. While she was preoccupied with one auction, he went and knocked on the door of the Jasper colonial, and made the owner a cash offer.

"There's a fine for breaking a contract with the auctioneer," the owner scoffed.

"I'll pay the fine," Ridge said. "And I'll make it worth your while."

The look on Casey's face when she beat him was worth showing up to see. And he thought it would be fun to throw her a curveball—but now he felt guilty. And childish.

He *had* been poking Casey in the arm, he realized, and promised himself he'd make things right the next time he saw her. It started as an innocent game of cat and mouse, but he'd taken it too far. If Randi were alive, she'd be ashamed. And Ash...

Oh Lord, Ridge silently groaned, *please don't let Ash find out how much I spent.*

CHAPTER 10

"Thanks for stopping at the Donut Den, Ms. Parks."

The girl behind the counter sing-songed to Casey while handing her a wax-paper bag, and told her to stop back soon.

Casey nodded her thanks and tried to smile, but knew it didn't reach her eyes.

Thanks to Ridge's Jasper house bombshell, there would be no celebration at the diner—even alone. No warm and gooey omelet or buttery toast. A single cold donut would have to fuel her drive and determination to succeed. The sweet chocolate frosting, she hoped, would take the bitter edge off her morning.

Ridge had whispered earlier that the Jasper house was his. Of all the things she'd like for him to whisper, that was not anywhere on the list.

Back in the office, Casey made a fresh pot of coffee and wondered what his game was—*why did he want these houses, really?* Ridge was only mildly interested in the little bungalow near hers and Ash's, and it required a lot of work. He ought to get on it.

Miss Emily had cared for it the best she could with her limited income, but it needed to be dragged into the current century—probably kicking and screaming. If it was anything like hers, the electrical needed updating from the old nob and tube wiring, and the foundation might need shoring up to hold the new, heavier appliances.

Her own roof was in good shape, but she wasn't sure about Ridge's bungalow. Casey could see that the flashing around the chimney had been compromised through years of extreme Wyoming weather. When she pointed this out to him, he just shrugged.

She and Ash were working hard to get their two of the *three bears* ready to rent, while Ridge had lost his interest in the project.

"The painter called with estimates for *three bears*," Amber said without looking up from her computer. The overhead light shone on the purple streak in her pretty blonde hair. Her fingers, clacking on the keyboard, were adorned with half a dozen silver rings.

"It might just be *two bears* if Ridge won't get on board," Casey said.

"Ash told me as much in our Econ class; said his dad used to come every day and bring him lunch or dinner. Or just show up to help," Amber said.

"I know," Casey said, pouring two mugs of coffee. "I think that's what appealed to me about buying the Madison house. The Wests just seemed so... nice."

Catching glimpses of Ridge West might have sweetened the Madison property in Casey's eyes, she could admit. But now he seemed more interested in beating her at her game. Only, it wasn't a game. It was her livelihood.

"Aw, did you dream that Ridge would bring you a sandwich?"

Maybe I did, Casey thought but didn't say. *A chicken salad sandwich on rye, with a slice of tomato, please. Pickle on the side.*

"How did he know about Jasper?" Casey stood in front of Amber's desk, setting down a mug of the fresh brewed coffee with a large spoonful of honey, the way her intern liked it.

"Thanks," Amber mumbled.

The intern barely looked up from her computer. When she did, it was because Casey put a bag on her desk with what she hoped was an apple danish.

Amber sighed and looked up.

"You didn't even *want* that old house on Jasper," Amber mumbled

33

while opening the bag. "It's on a corner lot, by the big church. You said they might complain if you added a fire pit and outdoor movie screen."

"It's not the house so much as the information about Jasper," Casey said. "Where did he get that?"

Amber shrugged again, but Casey knew the girl had lived in West Gorge her whole life, and must know something, so she waited.

"He's Ridge West," Amber said at last, through a mouthful of pastry. As if that explained everything.

When Casey still didn't let her off the hook, Amber continued, setting down the coffee and using her free hand to embellish her words. "He's Ridge *West* and this is *West* Gorge. That's the *West* River," Amber pointed. "And over there is the *West* hospital, and…"

Casey let her shoulders fall in defeat as she comprehended what Amber was saying.

"He knows people," the young girl said, shrugging just one shoulder. "And if he doesn't, he goes up to the door and tells them who he is. Who can say no?"

"Interesting."

"Who's going to stop him?" Amber asked.

Me, Casey thought. *I will stop him. I have to.*

CASEY FILED Amber's comments away for later—perhaps there was something there.

Her own strategy was textbook. She flipped smaller homes into profitable rentals when possible, and acted as listing agent for as many home sellers as she could. The more homes she put on the market, the more visible her name would be.

And so on.

Ridge once complained that by flipping the smaller houses, she was making it difficult for hard-working people to afford the entry-level homes—but here he was, doing the same. Maybe worse.

Had she picked the wrong town for her fresh start?

Was he really making her suffer for buying the Madison house?

Casey stewed while sipping her coffee. This was her doing, and she shouldn't be angry at anybody but herself. But she didn't like being bested by him, or any man. The last time that happened, the price tag had been steep.

It cost her everything. Her good name, her business, and nearly every cent she had.

CHAPTER 11

"*Y*ou're starting to look old. Grief is aging you."

The memory of Derek Vance's words still stung, years later. That he said them to Casey so soon after her father died, when the anguish of losing both parents had indeed carved lines of sorrow onto her soul and face, was unforgiveable.

Yet, she hadn't held him accountable. She allowed him to stay in her house, and in her bed, long after she should have kicked him to the curb.

It was herself she couldn't forgive.

If only she'd been stronger, or listened to her father and even her employees, she would have cut Derek loose at the first signs of his once sweet words turning sour, and unkind. Then he couldn't have stomped on her heart or ruined her business.

The mess she left behind in Phoenix was nobody's fault but her own, Casey knew. But there was no use looking back. All the "if only" sentiments only led to bitterness—and bitterness was for the idle. There was simply too much to do.

It took five full years to rebuild what Derek Vance destroyed. He'd been her business partner and a lot more, or so she'd imagined. When she realized how deeply she'd been fooled, Casey hardened her heart against trusting men. She resolved to love only her work, and make her career stronger than ever.

"You just gave him too much access," her lawyer told her as he explained how it was nearly impossible to go after Derek or recoup her losses. "We could try, but it would be a lengthy and costly battle."

The money was long gone and so was he, Casey figured. Probably out of the country.

"Idiot," she yelled to the heavens quite often, speaking to both herself and Derek. They were just starting to make some real money again after a dip in the economy, but he got restless and greedy. Derek never liked to wait for anything. So he drained their money—which was mostly *her* money, along with company funds—and bolted.

"Well good luck when it runs out," she would say to his face, if he had the guts to show himself. They both knew she was the brains of the operation. All he brought to the partnership was hollow charm, which she once saw as an asset to their business. Casey made it her goal to mentor Derek, and turn him into her perfect partner.

Her father warned her before he died. "I don't like him. I don't trust him," Daddy said, "and neither should you." The memory made Casey sad—she should have listened to his wise counsel, instead of falling for Derek's *flattery*, and saccharine-sweet sentiments.

After Mama passed, her father was her best friend, business partner, and life coach. He brought Casey into his business and before he died, signed everything over to her.

Their real estate agency in Phoenix was small but solid. Customers bought starter homes and then bigger homes. They also referred Casey and her father to their friends, saying, "you can trust these folks."

But her sweet dad, he didn't like Derek at all. With good reason, it seemed.

He and Mama had an exceptional marriage. Leaning on each other in good days and bad, they treated each other with grace and kindness until the very end. Casey vowed she would have a marriage like theirs.

Sadly, marriage with Derek didn't seem to be on the table.

It never even came up.

At her core, Casey was old-fashioned, and waited a long time for Derek to ask. She dreamed of her father walking her down the aisle, but that never materialized. Using his last breath, her father warned her one more time, saying the thing that hurt the most.

"You're worth more, daughter."

Grieving, Casey struggled to run the business. She relied on her stellar staff, and leaned on Derek more and more. A few years younger than herself, Derek bucked against the responsibility she tried to place on him. Like a street dog with a new collar, he grumbled and growled, taunted and sometimes outright *insulted*. He probably thought he was subtle—but to Casey, his words hit like a sledgehammer.

If she had an ache or a pain, he would comment that, *well she was getting older*. Or say she needed to stay in shape if she wanted to rob the cradle.

"Babe, can't you take a joke?" He'd quickly come to his own defense.

In the rearview mirror Casey saw how he twisted her objections around, making *her* apologize for *his* lousy behavior. She just wanted to keep peace in the family. That they weren't actually a family... well, Casey was the last to figure that out.

He wasn't all bad—at first.

Sensitivity hadn't been Derek's strong suit, and neither was business. But he was good to look at, and not a bad cook. After a few years together, they'd settled in like a couple of old shoes. Casey felt secure enough that she put his name on the business and bank account. She treated Derek with the utmost trust and respect, and hoped for the same in return.

When it failed, it was a tough lesson to learn. She'd never forget that any man was capable of smiling at her one minute, and ruining her the next.

Leaving Phoenix was the hardest thing she'd ever done. Her parents were buried there. The Parks' good name had been on a downtown sign for decades, until Derek dragged it into the mud.

Maybe she should have stayed and fought. But without her family or her business, she had no fight left in her.

So here she was in West Gorge, waking early, staying up late, and falling out of trees—driven to succeed by a sad combination of anger and humiliation.

Why Ridge West wanted to go head-to-head with her, she didn't know. He had more money and land than God. But she wasn't the same old *pushover* Casey Parks she used to be; Derek saw to that. She would need to dig deep, and show Ridge who he was tangling with.

CHAPTER 12

"*He* said *what?*"

"He said, he'd skip the cake," Kat answered Gunnar, "then asked for fresh fruit."

"Is he okay, do you think?" Gunnar looked concerned.

"He looks okay," Kat said, "maybe a little flushed. Otherwise, he looks well rested and seems to have more excitement about life than I've ever seen on his face."

"But why would my dad not have his favorite chocolate cake?" Gunnar wanted to know.

"Ridge said he wanted to lose a few pounds. He's watching his waist line."

Gunnar choked on his iced tea when Kat said that, and sprayed a little on the tiles. He went to get a towel to dab the floor.

"Keep your towel handy, cowboy," Kat said, "because there's more. Ridge also asked Liu to make him more *salads*, and fewer steaks."

Her husband was aghast, Kat could tell. But as a doctor, and the matriarch of a ranch full of cowboys, Kat was pleased. Her goal in hiring Liu was this very thing—it certainly wasn't for Liu to fall in love with Gunnar's brother Colton, and marry him. Though she was happy for the young couple, and loved her new sister-in-law like crazy.

But now, it was only a matter of time before Liu and Colton would finish building their house and have babies, and Liu would resign her position as ranch cook. As it was, the young bride had been struggling to keep them fed in the afterglow of their courtship and wedding.

Pride in her work was a motivating force for Liu, but Kat knew there was a million things Liu would rather do; open wedding gifts, for one. Or getting ready for their December honeymoon in Asia. And not the least of all, kissing her husband, who had gone to great lengths to win over the chef and her family this summer.

Liu's helicopter parents and grandparents had, at times, moved into the cook house to help with meal preparations. But the last thing Liu and Colton wanted was to share their honeymoon house with Ling, Zhang, Chun, and Tao.

To the Chen's credit, they respected Liu and Colton's space. Now, Liu had to navigate not only the Chens, but the growing West clan, too.

Kat understood.

After marrying Gunnar, she moved into the massive West home as one of the family. But one by one, they were leaving the nest, and it was okay. The transitions were healthy and happy. And Kat herself was growing more confident in running the home, accelerated by the arrival of baby Willow.

A league of regular housekeepers and contractors helped keep the ranch house and grounds in good repair. And a new ranch cook strictly kept the hard-working ranchers and cowboys fed in the outbuildings where they gathered each day for assignments.

Knowing everyone and everything was cared for, Kat could focus on her own research and hospital work, along with her growing interest in the West Foundation.

"The house is quiet," Kat said to Gunnar as they moved into the great room to take in the view of the gorge and the flowing river. The fall colors in Wyoming were at their peak, which were mostly yellow from the aspen trees. Growing up in the Midwest, Kat saw plenty of reds and oranges, too. But Wyoming had become home for Kat; the first home she ever wanted to be since her tumultuous childhood had soured that concept.

"No loud and jokey Colton," Gunnar agreed, "hard to believe he's gone; living with his wife in the cook house now."

"Pike's not coming back," Kat said. Pike and Paislee moved to a large modern farmhouse in a treed corner of the new housing development, complete with a guesthouse and studio.

Gunnar nodded.

"Ridge is gone a lot these days," Kat said, "and so is Ash."

"Their real estate business is keeping them busy," Gunnar said. "Not to mention it's Ash's last year in school."

"Maybe Ash's last few months," Kat said. "He might graduate early. He has enough credits and I don't think high school holds any nostalgia for him."

Gunnar nodded. He would remind Ridge to plan a college tour for Ash at the tail end of the harsh Wyoming winter. Ash was bright, with lofty goals. He hoped the boy's ambitions hadn't been dulled by being awarded his grandmother's estate.

Since being abandoned by his parents at a young age, and orphaned by the loss of his grandmother, Ash Gibson had become Ash West through Ridge's adoption. The boy had a few rough months as he settled in, but after meeting regularly with a therapist, he seemed to be flourishing.

Ridge gave him all the attention he needed, as well as space when that was needed. They had side-by-side homes that they were refurbishing into rentals, and Ash was doing well in his classes.

His future was bright, even though his past was painful.

And the West family fully embraced Ash as their long-lost little brother, complete with chores, pranks, high expectations, and overstuffed school lunches. He was a full heir to the vast West fortune, and Gunnar, Pike, and Colton took every opportunity to model for him philanthropy and responsibility to the community.

"I scheduled Ash's senior photo shoot," Kat said as they relaxed, "but he needs a new suit. Can you see to that?"

"Yep," Gunnar said. "Leather fringe jacket and bolo tie? Racoon-tail hat?"

"I was thinking charcoal wool with a silk tie," Kat said, knowing Gunnar was teasing. The West men, for all their love of the outdoors, knew how to clean up when it was called for. They were a handsome bunch with their sandy hair, and the height they inherited from their tall Nordic mother.

Ash was darker and leaner, but his good humor and kind heart were very much West.

"I thought he just got a new suit," Gunnar said, sleepily.

"He did, for Pike's wedding in Denver a year ago. It would not have fit for Colton's wedding," Kat said. "Thank goodness we all wore silks and linens for that event."

The celebrations for Liu and Colton had been a sort of Asian-Cowboy fusion. Kat loved adding the gorgeous wedding portrait to the family picture wall, featuring Liu in her lovely yellow chiffon gown and jade ring.

Sitting on the sofa next to Gunnar, she could feel him relaxing into an afternoon nap. His dog Jet was sleeping by the late September fire in the big stone fireplace, and the sky outside was cloudy and dark—rain would be coming in this evening.

Kat was grateful for the other Wests now on the ranch, as Rowdy had moved in to become the general manager. Lord knew he didn't need money. After selling his own ranch in Montana, he didn't need to add to his millions. He needed a purpose. Especially after leaving behind his professional rodeo career.

Rowdy's brother, Gray, also made Wyoming his home now. The pilot spent several months fighting wildfires, but bunked with Rowdy in the comfortable guest house when he could, and worked on the ranch. Both men talked of buying their own homes in town, or maybe having Colton build new homes in West Gorge Woods, his new development.

"I like having Rowdy run the ranch alongside you," Kat said in a hushed tone as she curled up with her head on her husband's lap.

"Mmm," Gunnar answered in his sleep.

"Are you dreaming of where to take me on a vacation?"

CHAPTER 13

"Thanks for coming over... *again*." Liu stood behind her cook table, chopping and prepping food for the West family meals. Sun was in Paislee's arms, where she'd been every day for the past week. "What would I do without you, Auntie Paislee?"

"No problem," Paislee said, rocking the baby to sleep after her mid-day feeding. She knew she should lay her down and encourage her to self soothe, but felt so sad for the motherless child. Paislee instinctively wanted to compensate for the baby's loss.

More and more, she found it harder to stay away.

That first day, she dropped the baby back home when it was her bedtime, giving Liu and Colton some peace and quiet. The next day, she found clothes and toys that had belonged to Willow she thought Sun could use. When she knocked on the door, Liu answered much like the previous day, with a sobbing baby in her arms. Paislee quickly quieted and fed her.

Now, Paislee arrived every afternoon during the "fussy hours" and took over so Liu could get some work done. She was a regular mother's helper—only Liu was not the mother, and Paislee was no teenager —she was a grown woman, and growing very fond of baby Sun.

"I'm happy to be here," Paislee answered Liu, who looked more rested than she had in days. "But you just tell me if I'm overstaying my welcome."

"Sit and eat, *zuòzhe chī,*" Liu told Paislee, setting a plate of spring rolls and vegetables in front of her, along with tea, "and tell me about the Arts and Culture Center—how are the plans coming along for the exhibits?"

Paislee continued to rhythmically pat the sleeping baby on the back while filling Liu in on her vision for a permanent exhibit of paintings by Pickford West, Ridge's grandfather and founder of the town and ranch.

"I've been getting the paintings cleaned and reframed," Paislee said, "though most were miraculously well preserved and protected from dust and sunlight, wrapped in Addie's quilts and such."

Liu nodded.

Getting to know Paislee was fun. Liu didn't have a sister, or brother. For years, her family poured their energy into just her. She embodied all the Chens' hopes and dreams. Which is why it was hard for them to accept her job as a chef, and her marriage to a very un-Chinese cowboy.

But like Liu, the Chens had learned to love the West family.

Listening to Paislee talk about art history and contemporary painters was really interesting for Liu. Pike, she knew, had a special painting for she and Colton to hang in their new home they were building. Liu also hoped to have one of Pickford's paintings, or at least a reproduction, in their home.

In the late 1800s, a very young Pickford had traveled by covered wagon to Denver City, then made his way to the Wyoming gorge—now known as the city of West Gorge. His artwork had been hidden away in an old family barn and cabin. If not for Pike and his love for the old buildings, they might still be lost.

The other thing Pike discovered there was his own passion for art and painting. Encouraged by his art curator bride, he now devoted his time to furthering his talent in their backyard studio.

"The old West settler's cabin was dismantled and relocated,"

Paislee said, "and will be assembled next to the culture center for school groups and history buffs to tour."

Liu nodded appreciatively. Her own ancestors settled in Wyoming around the same time, and had rich stories of their own to pass down. In the town where she grew up, there were small museums filled with photos and artifacts of the industrious Chinese settlers, so far from home.

"It's good when heritage is preserved for future generations," Liu said.

"Yes," Paislee agreed, "someday our own children will get to play in the settler's cabin of their West ancestors, Liu."

As she said this, she and Liu both gazed at baby Sun with the same thought: *her heritage is a mystery, and right now, so is her future.*

CHAPTER 14

"*K*eep it neutral. That's the ticket."

Ugh, did she really say 'that's the ticket'?

Casey's brain failed her, standing so close to Ridge in the Madison house. Her heart pounded like a drum. They were just looking at carpet samples and countertop finishes—this was not exciting stuff. Yet, the musky aroma of his aftershave was lassoing her, pulling her closer and closer.

The fact that he showed up unexpectedly this morning, ready to get to work on the bungalows, threw her for a loop. That he was being all nice and polite disarmed her, making her forget her resolve to beat him at his own game.

But maybe she would play along—for now, anyway. Her daddy always said you could catch more flies with honey than with vinegar. If Ridge was going to be on his best behavior, so would she.

"The berber carpet looks nice, but I think the plush is softer on the feet, and might wear better in the long run," he said. "What's your opinion?"

"Oh..." Casey fumbled for words, "my opinion. Let me think."

My opinion, she wanted to say, *is that with your shirt sleeves rolled up, your forearms look just as tanned and strong as I'd imagined.*

Casey watched Ridge's arms flex, and forgot all about unearthing his mysterious agenda. Instead, she fantasized for a minute that this same arm was reaching out to her, pulling her in against the warmth of his body. If he took the lead, she would follow. Wrapping her arms around his broad shoulders and tucking herself under the cleft of his chin, she'd eagerly wait for his gravelly voice to call her name.

"Casey..."

It was just how she'd imagined.

"*Casey?*"

"I'm sorry, what were we talking about?" Casey shook her head.

Ridge looked at her closely, slightly bemused. His eyes crinkled as they appraised her once again. She had to shove her hands in her pockets to keep from reaching up and touching the skin between his eyes and his silvery hairline—to see if it was as soft as it looked.

"Berber versus plush carpet. Quartz countertop versus the stone," Ridge said at last. "Are you okay? Need some water, or *food...* when did you eat last?"

The kindness of his questions took her by surprise.

"Casey, why don't we go have lunch." Ridge pointedly asked. "There's a new Tex Mex Grill on the edge of town I've been wanting to try," he went on, sounding nervous, "I'd love... for you to come with me."

Casey lifted her gaze to his sweet and earnest eyes and felt a flood of compassion for Ridge. He probably hadn't asked a woman any such thing in years. But they were just—what? They weren't friends, or enemies. The two had a reluctant partnership going, so maybe this was a business lunch.

"Sure," she said with a smile, standing taller. "I'm actually hungry, and hate to eat alone."

Casey kicked herself for being more honest than she'd meant to be, but the comment seemed to roll right off of Ridge. He opened the door for her—which she appreciated. When was the last time a man did *that?* And tentatively at first, his hand had rested lightly on the small of her back as she climbed into his Range Rover.

That felt very nice.

So did the leather seats of his four-wheel-drive. He kept his car pristine.

They were probably both a little jumpy, but it didn't take long to reach the restaurant where they were escorted by an enthusiastic host who treated Ridge like a rock star.

"Ridge West, well I'll be!"

Ridge deflected the attention by introducing Casey to the owner, and telling him to be sure and call her for any real estate needs. "And pass her name along. She's doing great things for West Gorge," he said, before tucking into a quiet booth.

This was a side of Ridge Casey had never seen—everybody's friend, and town booster. He wasn't manipulating, or conniving... he was merely supporting one new business, while also promoting hers. It almost made her sorry that she had to end his real estate career.

After ordering and taking a few sips of her iced tea, Casey smiled across the table. "Now, tell me, what great things am I doing in West Gorge?"

Ridge thought for a minute and smiled.

"Well, you sure do beautify this dusty old cowboy town."

Casey blushed at the compliment.

"I'm not letting you off the hook that easily, Ridge. When we were in jail..."

A few diners near the booth stopped talking and looked up in shock at her comment. Casey softened her voice.

"Not so long ago, in *jail*, you accused me of preventing the town's hard-working residents from being able to afford homes."

Ridge laughed a little and shook his head at the memory, which was all too clear. They had this unpleasant conversation while in the West Gorge holding cell, after getting caught taking unlawful sneak peeks at the little bungalow next to Ash's.

"I did say that, didn't I?"

Casey nodded and waited.

"Yet here I am, doing the same and worse." Ridge went on to tell Casey of his conversation with Ash, who accused him of overspending, and falsely driving up real estate prices. "And I know better."

"Why do you suppose you're doing that, Ridge?"

Because I want to be near you.

Because a little friendly competition makes me feel alive again.

Because of the beautiful sparks in your eyes.

All the things Casey longed to hear were interrupted by a jarring vibration; a notification had come in on her phone that was on the table in front of her. Glancing at the number, she swallowed a surprised gasp. And there's no way she could have disguised the fear.

CHAPTER 15

*R*idge West knew the look of fear in a woman's eyes.
All too well.

He saw it when his wife discovered the lump in her breast that seemed to materialize overnight; and again when she got the worst news possible from the oncologist.

Sure, he'd seen fearful looks on Randi's face through the years when one of the boys got thrown off his horse, or disappeared for a time without telling mama where he went.

The look on Casey's face fell somewhere between worry and cancer—it was real enough, but she hurriedly tucked her phone in her purse.

"Sorry about that." She lifted her coffee mug to her lips for a sip, then turned away to gaze out the window.

When her phone had pulsed, Ridge could detect the word Phoenix as the location of the caller. It was an easy word to decipher upside down. He hadn't meant to pry but it caught his attention, as phone notifications were meant to.

Lifting his own mug, he thought about Phoenix.

Years before, he and Randi took a rare road trip to Arizona. Just the two of them.

His wife's friend from the law school they attended in Michigan was becoming a judge, and Randi wanted to be at the swearing in. The boys were well into their teens, and driving themselves to school, so they left them in the care of their trusted cook and housekeeper, and set off for two full weeks.

Once they got out of Wyoming, they spent a few days in Colorado, meandering along the river into Utah. At Lake Powell, they rented a houseboat for five days where they putted along, in and out of the many fingers of the massive body of water. Several times each day they dove in to cool off, then huddled together in the chill of the evenings.

The red banks and cliffs along Lake Powell made for an endless display of dramatic shadows and vistas as the sun rose and set—their cheeks ached from smiling in wonder at the scenery. At night, the sky filled with shooting stars that illuminated the canyons and plateaus.

He hadn't thought of that trip in years, but was glad for the prompting. Randi's golden hair had taken on an ethereal glow from the sun, and wearing her tiny band-aid of a bathing suit, she looked more teenager than mother to three teens.

By the time they arrived in Phoenix, they were as close as newly-weds, holding hands and laughing at private jokes—when he asked Randi if, upon seeing her friend's success and prestige, she regretted the life she'd chosen, she merely smiled and rolled her eyes.

"As if," she said, obviously satisfied with her lot—which thankfully included him.

Ridge was the first of the two to break from the memories each had drifted off to. He found and held Casey's eyes with his own, waiting for some explanation, but there was none. She smiled as if the call was nothing at all—a wrong number, or some such fluff. But when she picked up her fork to continue eating her taco salad, Casey's hand was unmistakably trembling.

"Casey?" Ridge asked cautiously. "Everything okay?"

The urge to reach across the table and place his hand over hers was strong. If memory served, that simple act calmed the panic bubbling up in Randi Lynn on many occasions. But he wasn't sure that intimate gesture would be appropriate, or welcomed.

"Everything's fine," she lied. "Ready to go?"

He pushed the last of his burrito around on his plate and nodded, then signaled to pay the bill. Looking at her again, he opened his mouth to nudge her towards disclosing a little more about the call, but held back.

Casey Parks was a strange and beautiful closed book. Her cover was lovely and mysterious, and Ridge suspected her story was worth waiting for. In the meantime, he felt an old familiar feeling that he couldn't ignore—*protectiveness.*

They walked together to the truck, and as he opened and held the door for Casey to settle in, something caught the corner of his eye— an old blue Ford parked on the street. Ridge didn't recognize the car, but what made him look twice was the man behind the wheel. He had his window down, which was unusual on a chilly day. Then the man leaned out to take pictures with his phone—of them.

Not wanting to alarm Casey, Ridge tried to shield her as she settled in. Glowering, Ridge turned the key, hoping to swing past and note his license plate. But the man took off.

All Ridge managed to get was the first few numbers, and the state... Arizona.

CHAPTER 16

*E*VERY ENTREPRENEUR KNOWS THE FEELING... THAT MOMENT OF DESPAIR WHEN THE ONLY THING YOU ARE AWARE OF IS THE GIANT GAP BETWEEN WHERE YOU FIND YOURSELF IN THE LIFE AND BUSINESS YOU IMAGINE.

"AMEN," Ash West said to nobody—not even to his own ears. He wore noise-canceling headphones as he painted the trim in the kitchen of his grandmother's old bungalow. Most would suspect he was listening to country music, or rap. Instead, the audiobook of *What It Takes* by Schwarzman kept him company.

ASH WAS DETERMINED NOT to fail. He knew that the situation he'd fallen into with the Wests was God's grace, pure and simple. It was *undeserved favor*, as the pastor had defined it on Sunday morning. And yet, he was bound and determined to be equal to it.

The West legacy and mantra, which he had a legal right to claim as his own now, was to expand as opportunities arose. If they had the "bandwidth," that is; the definition of which was on his final business class exam.

Ash recognized that his own bandwidth was maxed out, what with renovating a house and finishing his last year of school. He also had responsibilities at the ranch, and shirking was not an option. His school counselor expressed to him that he might want to take part in more age-appropriate activities while he still could, such as attending a football game, or going to the Homecoming dance.

He told her he was considering going with his friend Amber to the dance. She worked for Casey Parks, one of his business partners.

"You know," the counselor said, "high school kids don't usually have business partners or colleagues. They have *buddies*."

Ash laughed at that, but assured her it was all good.

"My therapist thinks working on Granny's house helps me work through other things," he told the counselor. "We're both being restored, I suppose."

Indeed, the house was beginning to look a lot more inviting than when he'd inherited it—although in the past, on the good days when Granny still cooked her savory roasts and stews, there wasn't a more inviting place on earth.

She had taken him in as an abandoned boy, and loved him into healing—nearly, anyway.

Sometimes Ash wondered how his mother, who received the same love from the same woman, could turn out to be so cold and loveless herself. Leaving him in the middle of Wyoming, in the middle of the night, and running off to Mexico.

But he knew from his therapy sessions that these thoughts— constant childhood companions that they were—would take his hand and lead him straight down a path to depression if he allowed. So Ash forced himself to go through the mental exercise of moving his thoughts to the here and now.

Life was good, and not just on paper.

Ash truly loved the ranch, and the West family.

"I am part of the West family," he said aloud, removing the headphones after pausing his book. He hadn't heard the last chapter anyway.

"I belong. I am... *part of...* the West family," he said a little louder. "And they love me."

Taking a deep breath, Ash got up and pulled a cold ginger ale from the fridge and looked around. He was glad nobody was there to hear his therapy exercises. They sounded lame, even to his own ears, but they helped calm and center him.

But where was Ridge these days?

Not so long ago, his dad showed up nearly every day to help out, bring lunch, or keep him company. Now, Miss Emily's house languished and Ash worked alone as Ridge was off doing... what?

Gallivanting was the word that came to mind—one of his Granny's favorite words.

"Emily and I are going gallivanting," she'd say. "Don't wait up."

Ash smiled at the memory of happier days, when Granny could drive and knew where she was going when she did. She would take Emily to Cindy's Diner for the early-bird supper, or to bingo at the town hall. Or drive Ash to the mercantile for new jeans and shoes. This was long before the dementia set in, and he found car keys in his bagged lunch, along with an unopened can of beans.

Amber had a theory that Ridge was gallivanting with Casey Parks —her boss at the real estate office. Ash wasn't convinced, but he'd pay closer attention.

"It's okay," Ash said out loud, "Ridge is simply busy buying up the town. He hasn't forgotten about me. He won't change his mind about adopting me."

No, of course not, Ash thought with a smile. He put his head-phones back on and picked up the paintbrush once again, pushing down the anxiety churning in his stomach.

CHAPTER 17

"*Well hello, there, Arizona.*"

It didn't take long for officer Jason Scott to spot the old blue Ford, just a few blocks from the main drag.

He liked patrolling the streets of West Gorge. People being what they were, the mid-sized Wyoming town wasn't free from crime, but he and his team worked hard to make their presence known as men and women who expected everyone to behave.

No one was above law and order, not even the mighty West family.

That had been tested a few times. First, when Jason had to pick Ash West up for stealing purses in the nursing home. Being underage, Ash's stay should have been a few hours, max. But an early snowstorm kept the boy locked up for days.

Now, the only things Jason saw Ash lifting were heavy cans of paint at the hardware store. Jason stopped by the bungalow a time or two to check in, and even helped Ash change a complicated light fixture—happy to see the boy more gainfully occupied.

The most surprising West in his jail cell had been Ridge, when he brought him in for trespassing on private property and peeping into a dark window. It would have gone unnoticed if Casey Parks hadn't been inside the house, and the two hadn't tumbled over each other with their screams and clumsy falls.

When the call came from a neighbor taking out their trash, who heard "yells and all sorts of commotion" coming from an abandoned house, he expected to find bored teenagers—not the man who recently donated a new hospital and culture center to the town, and the pretty realtor who moved here a few years back.

But Ridge was a class act, and didn't hold the lockup against him. Just hours after Ridge went home with Gunnar, Jason was welcomed as a guest at Ridge's birthday bash at the ranch. They all laughed and ate cake like nothing happened.

No, Jason Scott wasn't sitting in anybody's back pocket. But when Ridge West called to ask him to keep an eye out for a suspicious character, he made it a priority.

"Old blue Ford, kinda beat up," Ridge said to Jason, "with Arizona plates."

Ridge thought he might be up to no good, and told Jason the man took pictures of he and Casey Parks with his phone as they came out of the Tex Mex Grill.

Wait, Ridge had lunch with Casey Parks?

Jason thought maybe Ridge was burying the lead, but he'd have to keep that gossip to himself—and especially away from his mother, Marta. She had a network of women in West Gorge that could spread news like a wildfire in a dry forest. And news about Ridge West dating *anybody* was up there with births, divorces, and the time the Episcopal clergy held their prayer retreat in Vegas.

THE CAR WASN'T hard to find.

Jason pulled up behind it and ran the plates. He thought it might be empty but when he got out, saw the driver had reclined his seat and was snoozing away. That gave him time to peek into the back seat.

When he rapped heavily on the driver's window with the business end of his flashlight, the man jumped and snorted. His mouth dropped open when he saw the officer, and he quickly returned his seat to an upright position and rolled down his window with a hand crank.

"Hands on the wheel where I can see them at all times," Jason said.

The man nodded and did as he was told.

"Officer, I…" he started to say.

"License, registration, proof of insurance," Jason cut him off. He shone a light on the man's face even though it was mid-afternoon, and only cloudy outside.

The man in the Ford opened his mouth to protest, but thought better of it and nodded. He reached into the glovebox for the pieces of paper, and used one hand to retrieve his wallet and license.

As Jason reviewed the information, the man started to speak again. "Did I do something wrong officer?"

"What brings you to West Gorge?"

"Sss… sightseeing," the man sounded unsure of his answer.

Jason theatrically looked around at the non-descript neighborhood, and raised his eyebrows at the man.

"Okay, I'm doing a job," the man tried again, more somberly.

"Can you prove that?" Jason asked.

"Not really," the man hemmed and hawed.

"Is it your job to take clandestine photos of upstanding West Gorge citizens? I'm getting complaints, and," Jason paused for effect, "I don't *like* getting complaints in my town."

At this, the man in the car bristled and frowned at the officer.

"Look," he said with a shrug, "truth is, I'm a private investigator."

"Licensed?" The officer held his hand out to review the official paperwork, but the driver of the old blue Ford shook his head in the negative.

"But unless I'm breaking the law, I'll be on my way."

Jason regarded the man, and chewed on the inside of his cheek.

"Funny you should mention the law," Jason finally said. "I was going to let you off with a warning, but I think I'll go review the town laws. Just so you'll feel you got the best service possible here in West Gorge. Keep your hands on the wheel, and I will be back shortly."

The man grabbed the wheel again, and slumped.

Jason got in his cruiser and turned on his flashing lights. Taking the lid off his coffee he slowly sipped, then ate his sandwich. After brushing away the last crumbs, he made a few phone calls. An hour later, and after half the population of West Gorge had driven by and gaped at the man in the blue Ford, Jason returned.

"This is a ticket for loitering, which is a hundred dollar fine," Jason told the man as he took the paper.

"*But...*"

"This is a second ticket for loitering within two blocks of a school. A five hundred dollar fine. Both are payable within 24 hours at the station downtown."

Red-faced and angry, the man opened his mouth to speak but thought better of it.

"And just so you know, we have lots of funny old laws that are still on the West Gorge books," Jason said as if he was chatting with a friend at a picnic. "It's illegal to play bingo for longer than five hours. It's illegal to have an uncaged bear in your backseat. You cannot sell a lightning rod without a license, and children can't have lemonade stands on Sunday."

Jason waited until the man in the Ford made eye contact again before continuing.

"You probably won't be guilty of any of those," Jason said. "However, the next time I see your car, I will impound it to run a Wyoming emissions test, which could take a few days. We only have a couple mechanics in town, and I think one is away on a fishing trip and the other is hunting in the mountains."

Holding the two tickets, the man nodded in defeat.

"Enjoy your sightseeing," Jason said before turning away. "The gorge is the other direction. After you pay your fines, I suggest you turn your car *thataway* and keep driving."

CHAPTER 18

"*P*aislee? Anybody home?"

The simple pleasures of married life were all Pike West needed to be happy. Walking the twenty steps from his studio to his house, and finding his new bride somewhere within the sunny modern farmhouse filled him with awe and wonder.

She was often in her office, curating for the new Arts and Culture Center that was being built. Sometimes she was hanging a new painting on one of their many empty walls.

And other times—secretly his favorite times—he found her lounging luxuriously on a plush sofa like a kitten in the sun, with a warm and welcoming look in her eyes at Pike's arrival.

Today, she was picking up toys and shushing him as he called her name.

"Baby's sleeping," she whispered, but walked over to wrap her arms around Pike's neck.

"For how long?" He asked with a smile, and a kiss on her neck. He encircled her tiny waist with his long arms and pulled her close. She answered his question with a kiss of her own, soft and feathery at first, then full on the mouth.

"You seem happy, Mrs. West," Pike said quietly once he could speak.

"Never happier, Mr. West."

A cloud passed over Pike's face that he hid by nuzzling her long silky hair. His wife was becoming very attached to little Sun, with almost daily visits to the cook house that turned into sleepovers at the farmhouse.

Paislee couldn't seem to stop pouring into the little orphan, and that was her nature, Pike understood. His wife loved fully and completely, without reserve. When he vowed a year ago to love, honor, and protect her until his death, he also made a silent vow to guard her tender heart against pain and breakage to the best of his ability.

But this situation was getting away from them both.

He couldn't tell her to stop falling in love with Sun, because she wouldn't—*couldn't*. She might resent him for asking. Since the day they married, Paislee had been a tireless proponent of his passions, encouraging him to paint and create, and make up for the years when he felt like a muzzled ox, with hands tied to the ranch. It was only right to encourage her passions in return.

This situation perplexed him though. How would Paislee deal with Sun being adopted by another family, or even by Liu and Colton? How well could she handle either scenario at this point? There were still many things he had yet to discover about his wife, but the depths of her attachments were no mystery.

"When is Sun going back to Liu?" He tried to ask this lightly, but felt Paislee stiffen in his arms, as if he'd mis-stepped.

"Tonight," she said, with a twinge of sadness in her voice. "Kat invited us to the ranch for a family dinner, and I'll hand off the baby there." Paislee sighed, and relaxed against Pike, seemingly defeated.

He held her tighter—he was embracing for one at this point.

. . .

AT THE RANCH, another new husband was walking on eggshells. Colton casually asked Liu when the baby was coming back to their house, and Liu tensed in his arms.

"Tonight," she said, tersely.

"Talk to me, Liu," Colton said in his no-nonsense style. "Does this make you happy, or not? Because this baby deserves something more than being in limbo, don't you think? Someone who is committed to her."

I don't like this limbo, either, Colton thought but didn't say.

"Yes, I agree," Liu said sharply.

"And if you want to raise the baby… if you want *us* to raise her, then that's what we'll do. Only…"

"Only?"

Colton stepped back from his wife and sat down at her kitchen island, so he could buy a few minutes and choose his words carefully.

"Only," he continued, "I want you to be sure this is what you really want, and not just feel obligated to do."

Liu looked closely at her husband. He had proven over and again that he could be trusted with her best interests. This carefree cowboy had shown a deeper, more committed side when he was wooing her than anyone she'd ever known. In return, he asked only for her love, and honesty.

"You've been raised to be an achiever, Liu," Colton said. "An overachiever in a lot of ways. And I think there's a part of you that sees little Sun as a challenge you could conquer if only you set your mind to it—like graduate school, the Suzuki violin method, or editing food videos. But this is much more complex than that, don't you think?"

Liu nodded at his words.

"I want to love her, and I know I would, given some time," she said quietly, sounding ashamed to hear such truths coming from her own lips. She had her husband to thank for that—his heart's desire was to see his young wife become in touch with her own feelings.

"Of course you would love her. We both would."

"I feel so torn, Colton. Should the baby be raised in a home that's part Chinese; where she'll know her heritage but where I have to learn to accept and love the... the *timing* of her? Or in a home that's not Chinese but where there's..."

Here Liu faltered with her words.

"A home... where there's *what?*" Colton asked gently.

Liu could only nod, as tears streamed down her face.

"Not what," Liu said. "But *who*. A home where there's Paislee."

CHAPTER 19

"*W*ait. You want to paint my house *pink*?"

Back at *three bears*, being nice to Casey was slipping away like a hand on a greased rope. as he met up with her and Ash to talk about exterior paint colors. The laughter he heard as he walked up to the Madison house set his teeth on edge, because he thought they might be laughing at him.

Seeing their growing friendship, a painful knot of jealousy twisted and turned in Ridge's chest, and he didn't like it. But maybe it was guilt. Ridge knew he hadn't been present for the boy the way he meant to be, and was reaping what he'd sown. Distance; in great abundance.

The three stood around a make-shift saw horse table looking at paint. Ridge agreed they should pool their efforts and have one house painter tackle all three jobs—the group discount was significant. But the colors were another matter.

"It's not really *pink*, it's in the white color palette," she tried to tell Ridge.

"Peony Blossom." Ridge could hardly say the words.

Ash turned his head away and Ridge was sure it was to swallow a smile, making him think their inside joke, earlier, had been at his expense. But maybe Ash was just trying to eat his sandwich. He was on his lunch break, and heading back to school before too long.

"Around these parts," Ridge said to Casey, "a man doesn't let a woman paint his house pink. And a woman doesn't ask him to bend on such an important matter."

"But Ridge," she stated her case, "three complementary colors will make the homes stand out on the street, and look fresh and new to prospects."

"I'm fine with that, Casey. I'd just prefer my house not be the ballerina of the bunch. I've got to show my face around town, still. Besides," Ridge said, looking at the two, "my home and Ash's home are not *Parks Place Rentals*. They shouldn't look like you own them."

Ridge noticed Ash and Casey glance at each other, and he realized he was right the first time. The two were in cahoots about something.

"That's... not exactly true," Ash said, uncomfortably it seemed.

"Is there something you want to tell me?" Ridge braced himself for news, and tried to keep his brow from furrowing. He reminded himself that he's the one who's been missing in action lately, not Ash. Maybe the high school senior has bitten off more than he can chew, and wants to put the project on hold.

"Casey offered to manage my rental as a *Parks Place*, at no cost," Ash said. "At least until I graduate, and have time to figure out what I'm doing." He added, "this way I can focus on my last year of school, and my grades. And what university I want to attend."

Immediately, Ridge felt hurt and jealous that Ash chose to talk with Casey about things they hadn't yet discussed. He tried not to show his emotions, because what Ash was saying made sense. Still he felt outnumbered.

"You get it, don't you Dad?"

"I get it. I get it, and that's mighty kind of Casey," he said to Ash, who exhaled the breath he was hanging onto. "I just wish you'd talked to me about it first."

Ridge hated airing dirty laundry of any kind in front of Casey, but it couldn't be helped.

"I would have," Ash said tentatively, "but you… haven't been around much."

Oof.

Ridge felt Ash's words as much as heard them, and they felt like a punch to the gut. He was aware of Casey's eyes on them both, and wished she'd excuse herself from this private conversation. She didn't need to be here, eavesdropping. But since she was, he'd reinforce for her that Ash was his boy—not hers.

Looking at the lad, growing in stature and confidence every day since Gunnar brought him home, Ridge forced himself to smile and place a reassuring hand on Ash's shoulder.

"You have a lot on your plate, *Son*," Ridge said, emphasizing the word "son" for Casey's benefit, lest she have any doubts who really had this boy's best interests at heart. "School should be your priority right now, so I wholeheartedly agree."

"That's exactly what Casey said," Ash said.

Ridge cringed uncomfortably at the words.

Oblivious, Ash smiled with relief as he gave his dad a quick hug then started for his Jeep. "Gotta run," he said. "Big Econ test today."

When Ridge realized Casey was standing right next to him, also waving to Ash, he quickly put his own hand down. They weren't a united front—they were *not* the American gothic couple, standing shoulder to shoulder with a hay fork and shared goals. Trying to be nice to Casey, he realized, had been a terrible mistake.

"You don't like me in Ash's business much, do you?" Casey turned to Ridge.

He snapped his head around in surprise at her question.

"Well no, as a matter of fact, I don't." Ridge looked at Casey head on. "You have no way of knowing his history, and what's best for him —and what's not."

Casey regarded Ridge's words, and nodded in contemplation.

"I know more than you think, Ridge West," she said. "While you're off climbing trees and ladders, buying up half the town, and coercing homeowners to sell to you…"

"*Coercing?*" Ridge sputtered at her words.

"... you're simply not around," Casey continued, ignoring his challenge. "Meanwhile, Ash and I are right here, working hard to protect our investments. And yes, he and I talk about all manner of topics."

"Such as?"

At this question, Casey closed her lips deliberately, and shrugged her shoulders. When she pantomimed zipping her lips and throwing away the key, Ridge knew the conversation was over. Putting on his gloves and pulling a knit hat out of his coat pocket, he grabbed his keys and got ready to leave.

"I see how it is," Ridge said, turning to face Casey squarely. "I steal your Jasper colonial, and you steal my son. We'll just see about that."

"And we'll just see who gets a pink house," Casey said under her breath after he'd gone.

CHAPTER 20

*D*erek Vance was eating off-brand taco chips in the hotel bed when the call came in from his private investigator. At least, Derek hoped the guy was a PI—he had a legit looking business card when they met in a bar one night. Derek was greatly relieved that the dude didn't skip town with the cash he'd given him.

And, it appeared he found the long-lost Cassidy Parks.

"Hang on," Derek had to pause the call to turn the TV off, and wipe the taco seasoning off his hands from his lunch.

Getting up to grab a towel, he caught his reflection in the mirror and wondered if Cassidy would even recognize him now that he was carrying a few more pounds, and wasn't so meticulous about his appearance. For a split second, he kind of missed the way she adored him, and cared for him. But this wasn't the time for regrets—he had a job to do if he wanted some more money to live on.

"I'm all ears," Derek said, settling in to hear what the PI found out.

She was going by *Casey* now, the PI said—not Cassidy.

That's why he couldn't track her down himself, Derek thought. She didn't exactly change her name, she was just using her childhood nickname.

Casey was making money and living well, it seemed.

"She looks different than the photo you gave me," the PI said. "Not so buttoned up or tightly wound. But it's her all right, and she's awfully pretty—maybe prettier."

Derek wanted to tell the PI to shut up about that stuff, and move on, but he supposed he was getting his money's worth of information. Maybe he just hated to hear that she was happy, and not miserable without him. Or miserable like he was most days.

The dude went on to say she was spending time in the company of the local billionaire. A fine upstanding widower who, Derek was certain, would be shocked to learn of Cassidy's—*Casey's*—walk of shame exit from Phoenix.

Derek himself knew he was directly responsible for her fall from grace. He smiled at how easy it had been to siphon all of the funds from their real estate company, and from Casey. And, Derek thought with an uncomfortable squirm, their employees—some who looked up to him as a friend.

But desperate times and all that.

He had been desperate. Derek thought back to when his *other* girlfriend told him she was pregnant. As soon as Casey found out, she'd kick him out of her house, and from the business, he knew. He would have been disgraced and broke.

So he just saved Casey the trouble.

She had to see it coming, though, right? Being an older woman and all. Casey wasn't that much older, maybe six years, and she was awfully pretty. But even though she was aging gracefully, as they say, she was still *aging*.

Derek had—until recently—managed through dumb luck and genes to retain his boyish good looks. The younger women had once flocked to him at the bars. The one who said she was with child was younger than himself, and much younger than Casey.

So he did what he had to do. He paid himself for all his hard work —and being charming was a marketable skill. Casey always told him how his charm had won over many of their home sellers into signing contracts, didn't she? Why shouldn't he get his payday, instead of leaving money on the table when she kicked him out.

Accessing the account, he took his past payments, current salary, and future payments—for helping to build the business and all. It was like taking candy from an older woman blinded by his good looks and charm.

He only felt a little bad, and whiskey took care of that.

No matter that the girl wasn't pregnant after all, and dumped him for a skateboarding punk who designed video games.

If he had to do it again, he wouldn't drain the joint account quite so brutally. He'd have left enough for Casey to cover the employee payroll and taxes—he may have gone too far.

Maybe.

And just maybe he wouldn't have blown the money so fast on trips, and that stupid sports car that broke down—the one he had no money to fix. There was just enough to hire the private eye; the idiot who got in trouble with the local law in the town where Casey moved —the idiot who was going to send him an invoice for his tickets.

Yeah, don't hold your breath, buddy.

But the idiot did find out about the billionaire, the one who gave him something to hang over Casey's head.

Derek took a swig from the bottle and called a long familiar number. He didn't expect Casey to answer. It was enough for her to know that he was back.

And if she didn't play ball? Of course she'd play ball, as long as there was a threat of anybody finding out about her disgraced name. Her name was valuable to her, more than anything. If not? Then let the new guy see what he's getting himself into, unless Casey wises up and cuts him in on the scam she's running.

Oh wait, Derek thought, she didn't run the scams. *He did.* But he's the only one who knew that, and Casey of course. But who would believe her? Not the widower, or his kids. Or the precious town that looked up to him.

Her secrets were safe with him, if she gave him what he wanted.

CHAPTER 21

*B*ack at her apartment, her head was absolutely spinning. *Spinning.*

The two things Casey swore would never happen, happened at the exact same time. Like a head-on *collision* that left her dizzy and confused.

The first unlikely event was when Ridge West showed up out of the blue, and acted nice. He actually asked her out to lunch, meaning he was willing to be seen in public with her, eating a meal. Not picking out paint.

They sat in a booth like two civilized people, with forks in their hands instead of knives in their backs.

The other impossible event was a phone call from Derek. *That* Derek. The Derek she used to defend against the attacks of her parents, and innuendos made by her employees.

No, he's not living off of my money.

No, he didn't charm his way into his position.

Then suddenly, painfully, no turned to *yes*. It was all true. Every bad thing anyone ever said or thought about Derek turned out to be true. He was a loser to the bone.

He made Casey believe he wanted to be her partner in work and in love, and then stuffed her life, good name, and respectability into a sack and snuck out of town. Just like that green cartoon character who tried to steal Christmas. Only, he didn't give everything back, or say he's sorry.

In Casey's version, he left *her* holding the bag of lost trust, unpaid payroll, and financial ruin. Capped off by a newspaper photo of her supposedly "skipping town." Who wouldn't look guilty under that lens?

For days and weeks after, Casey jumped every time her phone rang, wanting to hear from him—wanting to know why he did what he did. A time or two, her own fingers hovered over the phone as she thought of calling him.

"Hey Derek." She would be cool and casual if he answered, but never could bring herself to dial. He didn't call her either. Casey was left to figure everything out all by herself.

Weeks of denial at what he'd done turned into months of hatred, a solid year of sorrow, and a few more years of apathy.

In recent years, all the bad emotions were slowly replaced by a sense of satisfaction in her career, a happiness about living in Wyoming, and a general feeling of hope. Going on her first *sort-of* date with Ridge West was a natural next step. Seeing Derek's number appear on her phone was not.

You okay, Casey?

She lied to Ridge, but he saw through her.

Derek used to chide her for her non-existent poker face in real estate. She never could make a buyer believe they had to jump on a deal, before it went away. She couldn't lie to sellers about her sketchy competitors. Casey never wanted to do any of those things when Derek encouraged her to be less than ethical.

"Babe," he'd push, "everyone lies through their teeth in business —trust me."

Just the memories took her back to the years of hate, a place she didn't want to be, ever again. Yet here she was, mooning over a man who may not be any more ethical than the last awful fellow. Did Ridge lie and cheat? People said he didn't; she'd like to believe he didn't. He was assertive at times, but so was she—she had to be.

She didn't trust her own judgment, that was the problem. How could she trust Ridge?

"I just have to find out."

Casey started to noodle on a plan that would prove Ridge West's character once and for all; to see if he could pass the *Derek* test. Good or bad, she had to know the truth up front. She would never be blind-sided again like she was in Phoenix.

An innocent test, that's all it would be. A tiny little trap. And if the mouse took the bait, so be it. She would walk away from Ridge for good, and maybe the town. The thought of starting over was tiring, but so was letting Ridge run rings around her business and her emotions.

As for Derek, the best thing Casey could do was ignore him until he went away again—she had nothing left to give. She already handed him her life and dignity on a silver platter. What more did he want?

Oh, she had a little money in the bank once again. But most of her funds were tied up in her properties. Whatever she made from selling a flipped house or from a vacation rental, she invested back into her business. She bought properties for as little as possible, unless a certain cowboy drove up the price. In a moderately healthy economy, she'd get a good return on her money.

It was a long game, and a lot of effort, simply to have a modest retirement someday. A little house, a vacation every winter to some-place warm, that's all she asked.

Casey did have an ace in the hole, the one thing she never told Derek about. In a sea of dumb mistakes, her one smart move was hanging onto her parents' house and never telling him that she owned it free and clear.

The structure itself was nothing special, but the location was a hot spot. While a couple of school teachers in Phoenix deposited rent in a bank account each month, the unassuming home sat in a flourishing hub of restaurants, wine bars, and pricey condos, quietly appreciating in value.

Just the other day, a generous offer came in from a coffee shop chain. That income alone would replenish her savings, and allow her to breathe a little easier about her future. But the house would be torn down, and Casey wasn't quite ready.

Sometimes her mind still played a trick, telling her, *"Mom and Dad are waiting for you to come home,"* which she knew was nutty. Casey sighed and dropped her head in her hands, exhausted. Would the nightmare of her past ever end?

Until it did, she'd keep Ridge West at arm's length. As much as she was *starving...* absolutely famished for his nice guy act, she couldn't drop her guard—not until there was hard evidence that proved she could trust him.

Or not.

CHAPTER 22

"*I* think you were onto something, Amber," Casey's assistant was packing up and getting ready to head home as Casey got back to the office in the late afternoon.

"Okay," Amber said, not sounding interested or convinced.

"You're the one who said Ridge West was bullying locals into selling."

"Nope. I don't recall saying that. I did not use the word *bullying*."

"Suggesting… bullying…" Casey said, "it could be the same thing, really."

Amber shook her head. "Don't let the principal at West Gorge High hear you say that. He would strongly disagree, and we'd be back in the gym for yet another lengthy assembly on the topic."

Throwing her backpack over her shoulder, Amber smiled tiredly and told her boss she'd be back the next day, after classes.

STEPPING out on the streets of West Gorge, Amber inhaled deeply, breathing in the crisp autumn air. Her nostrils stung; there was snow on the horizon, she could tell. The locals could always tell. Thankfully, it was a few short blocks to her house.

Her mother sent a photo earlier of the roast she had in the oven, complete with "taters" and lots of carrots, the way she liked it. In the picture, Amber could see the beef cooking in an old beat-up pot that was her grandmothers. The girl smiled, thinking of the fancy enamel Dutch Oven she had hidden for her mother's Christmas gift.

Wish I could text you the smell, her mom had said, which made her smile.

Amber could only imagine the aromas that would welcome her in just minutes. She'd throw on her PJs and robe before dinner, and stay awake long enough to finish her homework. After that, she had to check *Amber Waves* for purchases, or comments on her items. Being a business owner was more work than she imagined, but reselling her vintage "finds" gave her a nice little bank account.

Casey was generous, too.

But walking along, Amber wondered if she should have gone with this internship—or accepted the offer from *Pet N' Feed*. Bunnies and puppies had to be less drama than real estate, and Casey Parks.

Yes, she got extra credit for her AP business class. And yes, Casey paid her much more than if she were cleaning rabbit cages and hauling bags of kibble. But sometimes she felt like a nanny to a couple of out-of-control kids.

Was she the only one who noticed how crazy Casey was for the widower, Ridge West, or how he was sort of nuts in return? She saw him at the auctions—he couldn't take his eyes off her boss. He drove Casey to distraction. The whole situation reminded Amber of stories about her parents' own school days. Back when boys and girls, and *yes*, to Amber's horror they actually referred to themselves as "boys and girls," couldn't seem to say, *hey, I like you.*

Instead, they'd embarrass and aggravate each other, like Casey and Ridge were doing.

Amber was so glad to live in an enlightened age, when it was no big deal to ask a guy to a party or dance. If he said yes, then cool. If he said no, that was cool too.

She recently asked Ash West to the homecoming game and dance, "as friends," she'd quickly added, so he wouldn't feel pressured. He was thinking about it. Amber hoped he wouldn't take too long. It was their senior year, and she didn't want to miss any more fun than she already had by working so much.

But Ash was a serious dude, with a drive to succeed not commonly found in a teenager. Plus, he had some ghosts from losing his gramma. If he said no, she'd give him a pass and they'd stay friends. She wouldn't devise a diabolical trap, or sabotage his life.

Sheesh.

IN THE QUIET of the office, Casey sat back with the little West Gorge newspaper, looking for inspiration. If Ridge was going to get creative with his tactics, she'd have to do the same.

Let's see, birth announcements could mean a bigger home. Retirement announcements could mean a smaller home or vacation home. Weddings meant a starter home.

Gazing out the window, she saw Amber down the road, walking home in the cold wind. She refused a ride, saying she needed the bracing air.

Ridge enjoyed the cool mountain air too, Casey thought. She saw the way he filled his lungs with it so regally when they were outside— like the other day, at the tri-level auction. The clean air seemed to heal Ridge, and center him; making his eyes and skin shine with robust good health.

In her mind, the freshness embedded itself in the collars of his shirts, and she longed to bury her face in the cottons, flannels and chamois fabrics to drink it... *him*, in.

He made a move towards her at last, asking her out to lunch. It wasn't a date, just a starter; an olive branch. Ridge was being kind—he probably took every hungry vagrant to lunch. So she couldn't let her guard down, even a little. Not as long as he was still going after everything she wanted with a vengeance.

She doubted she could ever trust him, but wanted to find out. How, though?

"Everybody knows him, and if they don't," Amber had said a few days before, "he goes up to the door and tells them who he is. Who can say no?"

Who indeed?

Maybe it was time to find out. If she dropped a hint and sent him on a wild goose chase, no one would be hurt, she was sure. She just wanted to see if he took the bait. But what house, and what home-owner? That was the question.

Reading the paper again, Casey got to an article in the back near the coupons and ads, and a seed of an idea began to sprout.

"That's it," she shouted out loud, slapping her hand on her desk.

It was perfect, she knew—and a little *awful.* There was no way he'd even touch it. But if he did… she'd have her answers. Picking up the phone, Casey dialed before losing her nerve. "Ridge, I'd like to apologize in person for our… misunderstanding."

Casey was glad the call went to voicemail.

"Meet me for coffee tomorrow?"

CHAPTER 23

"*A*gain, Ridge, I'm sorry."

Ridge watched Casey's face as she spoke, and she seemed sincere. They were sitting in a booth at the Donut Den, with mugs of cooling coffee between them.

"My own father meant the world to me," she said, quietly, "and I swear, I would never come between you and your son, or undermine your... guidance."

Ridge nodded, and softened his hard expression.

"Thank you for that," he said. He'd like to know more about her father, and would make it a point to ask when the moment was right.

"Ash and I do talk sometimes," Casey continued, "about nothing of consequence. Business, mostly. I should have asked you first before offering to help manage his rental."

"No, that's his call to make," Ridge said. "I was mad at myself for not being around more, and I'm afraid I took it out on you. It seems I've been doing other things, instead of keeping my commitments."

But that's about to change, he thought to himself.

Casey's face softened. She opened her mouth to speak when a waitress came to refresh their coffee mugs, and deliver their bacon and tomato sandwiches.

Ridge smiled across the booth at Casey as they ate together in companionable silence. This was the second time they were out in public together, sharing a meal.

It was nice.

He'd barely noticed her when she first came to town. It wasn't long after Randi had passed, and his mind was elsewhere. Memories from those days were sad and bleary. But if he recalled correctly, her stiffer suits made her look like an insurance agent.

Now, though, she wore softer shirts that hugged her. Ridge wondered if that was the only thing hugging Casey Parks. He never saw Casey with anyone except Amber. She didn't show up at the regular social events—the Spring Thaw, the harvest parties, the ranch cookouts or church picnics—events that brought people together.

Ranchers in Wyoming depend on these since their properties are so far apart. But newcomers are always welcome.

As Casey stirred cream and sugar in her coffee, Ridge admired the way she made a soft plaid shirt look as though it was painted on with a flannel-tipped brush. At her pearl-buttoned cuff, she wore a delicate gold watch and a ruby studded tennis bracelet. This was her only jewelry, besides a pair of understated earrings, and a hammered silver band on her right index finger.

Her jeans were snug, but not super tight. Casey's jackets were worn and soft, but flattering to her figure and lovely face. She always looked good as they walked together through stores, broke into abandoned houses, or climbed maples, he thought with a smile.

She could fall out of his tree any old time.

Casey smelled nice, too. He liked her understated ways and rustic elegance. Some women were too flashy and off-putting with their strong perfumes and makeup.

Everything about Casey Parks said there were treats and delights to be had if she ever allowed a man to get close enough. It wasn't the first time Ridge wondered how close she'd let him get—and he was starting to realize just how badly he wanted to.

But the signals she sent were wildly mixed. He saw the way she glanced at him sometimes, and it was nothing short of primal. Her body yelled, *Get close to me, Ridge*; while her eyes said, *Not with a ten-foot pole.*

Even so, Ridge thought maybe it was time to take a chance on Casey, and ask her out on a real date—dinner and a movie, or a romantic walk by the gorge. If she agreed, he'd talk to Kat and get suggestions. If she said no, well, he'd say he misread the signs, and hopefully they could remain friends and business partners.

"Casey, I…" he started to say, when she spoke at the same time.

"Ridge, I…"

He gave a *ladies first* gesture so she would continue.

"I want to ask your advice," she stated.

"Oh?"

"West Gorge real estate is a tough nut to crack, as you've been finding out. Getting to the inner circle of listings is next to impossible."

Ridge nodded, sure that she was right. There were lines of loyalty drawn around family histories, church affiliations, and business partnerships, to name a few entanglements that went back decades.

"I caught a whiff of a rumor about a house going on the market soon, over on Wright Street. All I know is this: it's a pristine Craftsman bungalow, owned by a prominent family. I'd like your advice on getting the listing."

Ridge took a sip of his coffee and contemplated for a minute. He knew the house, but it didn't make sense—the only Craftsman on Wright was owned by the Shire family. He knew Bud Shire, the town pharmacist, and his family quite well. Their daughter Daisy Shire owned Painted Bird, the popular gallery in town. Daisy was a friend to both Kat and Paislee.

Then there was Daisy's twin, Darlene Shire.

The wayward, free-spirited reporter had been Gunnar's girl for a year or so, and nearly became Ridge's own daughter-in-law. He shuddered to think of anyone taking Kat's place, and silently thanked God for the hospital shut-down that forced his son and Kat to fall in love before Darlene could get her hooks in Gunnar.

"Are you sure about that?" Ridge asked, not bothering to hide the skepticism in his voice. He didn't want to say, but he and Bud served on committees together—and Bud was essential to the community. Ridge didn't think he'd up and sell without first bringing in a new pharmacist for the town. That wasn't like him.

"Mm hmm," Casey said, sipping coffee and looking distractedly out the window.

"How could…?"

Ridge stopped himself from cross examining Casey, recognizing in his voice the same tone he'd used at the Madison bungalow. But Casey couldn't possibly know more about the Shires than he did.

He narrowed his eyes and looked closely at Casey, who was being evasive.

She was up to something. But what?

Building a relationship with Casey Parks was one step forward, and two steps sideways—like a dance. It made him second guess whether she was the right partner.

CHAPTER 24

*B*ud Shire and his wife meticulously maintained and improved their unique West Gorge home over the years. The woodwork gleamed and the painted trim was impressive. If they were to sell, Ridge thought, he'd want to buy it. Standing on the covered front porch, he could picture himself sitting on the cypress swing and waving to neighbors.

Maybe it was time to have a house in town, for those winter days when the ranch road was just too long and blustery.

One thing he wouldn't do was offer the Shires more than the house was worth—he'd learned his lesson. He'd help Casey get the listing, and then buy it through her if he so desired.

Walking up to the door, Ridge wondered if it was a bad idea to blindside Bud, but if the man was truly leaving town, and leaving the pharmacy unattended, the community had a right to know.

"Ridge," Bud said in surprise, "how are you?"

Bud stepped out onto the porch, and indicated they sit down. "I'd ask you in, but my wife is steam cleaning the carpets. *I'm* barely welcome inside when she's doing that."

Ridge smiled and sat down on a comfortable wood slat chair. The deep overhang of the porch provided ample shade on a sunny day, and a safe haven to watch the rain fall during the shoulder seasons.

"It's a beautiful house, Bud," Ridge said. "A real gem."

"We like it," Bud said. "Of course, we like it better now that Darlene moved out, and Daisy has her own place. Unlike your sprawling ranch, our four walls were closing in on us as the girls grew up."

"They're doing well?" Ridge was stalling.

"Sure are," Bud said. "Daisy's gallery is selling more art online than in person. She'll be working with your Paislee over at the new Arts and Culture Center, when it's complete."

Ridge knew the Arts and Culture Center would add a much-needed layer of art and history to the town, and entice more visitors.

He noticed Bud said nothing about Darlene. "Is there... something you need, Ridge?" Bud asked. "A prescription filled? I'll be back in the store shortly."

"Naw," Ridge said, "It may be none of my business, or just a rumor, but I heard you might be selling and moving."

Bud looked genuinely surprised. Either he wasn't going anywhere, or didn't think anybody knew. "Well that's news to me. Of course, my wife may be planning to sell, and giving me the boot," Bud laughed a little, "but she seems happy enough with me these days."

Ridge was relieved.

"Since we're dropping rumors over the fence... *I* have heard," Bud went on carefully, "you've been knocking on doors and offering folks more money than their homes are worth. If that's the case, I'd have to seriously consider it. Otherwise..."

Ridge cringed at Bud's words.

"I swore just yesterday those days were over," Ridge said, "but this house is one of a kind, Bud. If you and the missus ever want to sell, call me first." And then he realized what he was saying. "Or better yet, call Casey Parks to be your listing agent. *Then* I'll gladly pay you more than the house is worth."

The next time he saw Casey, Ridge would tell her the rumor had been wrong—they weren't selling just yet. But he'd already put in a word for her to get the listing if they did.

Bud smiled and shook Ridge's hand. "It's a deal. Now, if you don't mind, I'd better get back to the carpets."

Ridge stood up and said his farewells, looking one last time at the tree-lined street. Had he looked a little farther down, he would have seen Casey Parks sitting in her idling car, behind oversized sunglasses —watching in disbelief as the men shook hands.

CHAPTER 25

"*I* didn't actually tell a *lie*," Casey told herself as she sat in her car, staking out the Shire house. "I *inferred*, and there's a difference."

Instead of telling Ridge outright that the Shire bungalow was going on the market, she let him draw his own conclusions, thinking she'd still be able to sleep at night.

An ad in the West Gorge newspaper had been the catalyst. Casey saw an article congratulating Bud on thirty years of owning the town pharmacy. It featured a photo of Bud and his wife by their house, and Casey quickly formulated her plan.

Why then did she feel guilty? She merely tossed the chum into the ocean—Ridge was the actual shark that glommed onto the bait. Didn't that prove he'd stop at nothing to beat her?

She almost turned the car around and went home, thinking she'd never see Ridge walk on Bud's path and knock on his door. When he did just that, she was devastated. Casey caught him in the act. The man she was falling a little in love with was just as disappointing as the last guy.

"Wow, just wow," Casey yelled as she drove back to the office. "He just couldn't wait to run over to the Shire's house and grab the listing."

She wanted to be wrong about him, but Ridge failed the test. As soon as she dangled the juicy prospect in front of his greedy eyes, he ran as fast as he could to get it for himself. He would never lay down his competitive ways and let her make a living.

She could never trust him. Or count on him.

Back at the office again, Casey threw her purse on the desk, and opened desk drawers just to slam them shut. When Amber came in, Casey told her what had happened.

"So let me get this straight, you made up a listing…"

"Pretty much."

"And told Ridge about it…"

"I *inferred* really, but yes."

"Then he beat you to the *fake inferred* listing."

"He sure did."

"And you're mad."

"Oh, I'm mad."

CHAPTER 26

"*H mm hmm hmm baby... in the hmm hmm...*"

Paislee found herself humming what she realized was *Rock A'bye Baby* as she made her bed and got dressed. Before going down to the kitchen to prep dinner, she stopped in the nursery and smiled.

"See you soon, Sun," she said to the empty crib. The room was tidy and ready for a tiny guest to come over for a play date or nap, maybe even a sleepover if Paislee was lucky. The dresser drawers were filling up with new blankets and sleepers, little diapers, and even soft and chewy rattles.

It was so much fun shopping online for a baby—especially a baby girl. Paislee knew she really should stop; it was too much for the short spurts the baby was at the farmhouse. But how could she, when those little checks and florals were staring her in the face on her computer?

As she did nearly every day now, she planned her day around driving to the ranch and helping Liu with the baby. It had become such a routine that she no longer asked or called. She just showed up.

Liu left the door unlocked for her, and she let herself in. Usually late in the morning. That's when Sun would fuss inconsolably, and when Paislee would swoop in and take over. The little one never failed to relax, and serenely allowed Paislee to rock her to sleep, or read her a few books.

Paislee thought her sister-in-law was happy for the reprieve, and she admired Liu's *detachment*, for lack of a better word. She wasn't at all prickly about the baby's preference for her. Paislee thought she herself should be more detached, to protect her heart from breaking if and when the Chen's found a more permanent home for the baby.

Just the thought made Paislee's heart drop into her stomach, and her stomach, in turn, roll around like a sagebrush tumbleweed on West Ranch.

Pike was concerned about her, she knew. He was always happy to see Sun, but couldn't hide his protectiveness over his bride. Paislee loved him all the more for it.

"It's a good day for a slow-cooked stew," she said minutes later, standing with Pike in their large farmhouse kitchen. He must have noticed her from his studio, she thought. With her new schedule, he often came in mid-morning to see her before she left for the ranch.

Today, he brought a great gust of cold wind and the aroma of winter with him. He pulled out a stool from under the counter, and sat while she stood at the island chopping onions, carrots, and celery.

"Or," he said, taking his first sip of the fresh coffee she brewed for him, "it could be a perfect day for you and I to take a drive out to the settler's barn."

"You can't be serious," she said with a smile. "There's weather coming soon—we could get snowed in again."

"Would that be so bad?"

Paislee abruptly stopped chopping and saw a mischievous grin on her husband's face. *No*, she realized, it would not be bad to be snowed in with Pike, in the barn where they first fell in love and later enjoyed a wintry honeymoon together.

For three luxurious months after their Denver wedding, they had taken their time getting to know each other in new and wondrous ways. They didn't bother winding the old clock, for time had no meaning for them. Only the wood on the fire, the candles on the nightstand, and the snow falling outside—snow that eventually turned to spring rains—held any significance for Pike and Paislee.

Just thinking about those days stirred up warm red embers inside Paislee as she thought back to their first married months of discovery, and deeper love than she'd ever known. Lost in her memories, she looked up again and saw the same unmistakable love in Pike's eyes, as he held his arms up for her to walk into.

Pushing down her desire to see Sun, the piled-up workload for the arts center and the un-chopped carrots, Paislee held her husband's gaze and walked into his waiting embrace.

"My sweet Paislee," Pike whispered as he untied her apron and let it fall to the floor.

CHAPTER 27

*W*alking into Ash's little bungalow, Ridge felt odd. He began to realize how much his youngest had accomplished on his own, while he'd been off doing other things. With other people. He could only hope Ash would forgive his staying away.

"Dad!" Ash seemed surprised to see him. His delight quickly turning to agitation.

"You're coming along real nice here," Ridge said, pointing to the freshly painted walls.

Ash nodded tersely, "yep."

"Floors look good."

"Yep."

"I just hope you're not working too hard," Ridge ventured.

"My business goal is to be listed as a rental by the spring," Ash said.

"I see," Ridge nodded.

"What's *yours*?"

"Say what?" Ridge had been walking into the kitchen, but turned to face Ash.

"What's your business goal, Dad?" Ash had an edge in his voice. "Is it to build a real estate empire, or to disparage and undermine Casey Parks?"

"What are you talking about, Ash?"

"Amber told me Casey gave you a lead on the Shire house, and how you tried to steal the listing from her."

"There was no listing to steal, Ash." Ridge said evenly.

He was right, Casey had been up to something, Ridge thought.

"You didn't know that, Dad," Ash continued, his anger growing. "I never took you for someone so underhanded; a man who would crush the spirit of such a nice woman; a woman who obviously has trust issues. Casey is our *friend*. She's my friend, anyway."

Ridge turned sharply towards Ash at this comment.

"Trust issues? How do you know Casey has trust issues?"

"How do you *not* know, Dad? It's written all over her face. I guess it takes one to know one," Ash said, implying his own wounded past.

Ridge felt crushed himself at Ash's words, and his shoulders slumped as he leaned hard against a wall. Seeing his dad's face, Ash felt sorry he'd spoken so harshly to him.

"Dad, sit down," Ash said in a kinder voice than before. "I shouldn't have been so hard on you, and I'm sorry. Please sit down."

He brought Ridge a folding camp chair and motioned for him to sit down. Ridge's sore knee and deflated spirit must have been evident. Handing Ridge a bottle of cold ginger ale, he placed a hand on Ridge's shoulder and caught his eye.

"No, I deserved it," he told his son, sitting down but waving away Ash's apology.

Stepping back, it all made sense. He could see how she hadn't let her guard down because he kept coming after her livelihood like a battering ram. What choice did she have but to put up her dukes and fight back with a silly prank—was that *a test*; a trap?

Ash was right, he should have been more of a friend. Not an adversary.

"You haven't been here in a while," Ash said after Ridge took a gulp and nodded his thanks.

When Ridge spoke, his voice was thick. "I'm sorry."

Ash smiled at his dad.

His therapist encouraged him to open up more about his feelings, and not keep them bottled inside. That's when he got into trouble, acting out and all. He wanted to tell his dad he was tired of him chasing houses, and aggravating Casey. And he was tired of him being gone all the time—he liked having his dad check in on him, bring him a sandwich every now and then. It showed Ash that Ridge was thinking of him, and that meant the world.

"All I need Dad," he wanted to say, "is one person to be present in my life, and stay."

Just one.

"I've missed you, Dad," was what he landed on in the meantime. Simple words that had taken him years to speak.

CHAPTER 28

I'm not late, not really.

    Paislee pushed down the panic and calmed herself as she drove to the ranch.

She and Liu had no formal agreement—only a few weeks of routine. And routines changed all the time with babies. Still, she felt guilty for arriving slightly later than usual.

Paislee was very private, and would never even hint at what kept her home this morning. Although if anyone understood, it would be newlywed Liu West. But really, she and Pike had only married a year before. There was still so much to learn about each other, and so many lovely surprises.

My sweet Paislee.

The way he beckoned her with his eyes brought her back to the first time she ran into him at an art show in West Gorge—literally. His hands shot up and steadied her after patrons in the crowded room pushed them together. For a brief and wonderful moment, it felt like they were dancing.

Her life changed that night, and it's never been the same. She had been far from home, chasing answers—chasing the elusive *P. West*—

and found much more than she was looking for. At the same time, Pike unlocked a few mysteries of his own.

Together, their life was truly magical. Sometimes Paislee wondered if they should keep things the same, with just the two of them. But when she held little Sun, it gave her a glimpse of how love can expand and grow in a family.

"Should we keep things the same, Pike?" Paislee asked recently. "Is it wise to mess with perfection, do you think?"

He laughed a soft answer, "we'll have perfection as long as you're in the equation."

But went on to say what she knew in her heart, that as long as they were committed to each other, life would only get better and better, no matter what.

Driving through the massive West Ranch arches, Paislee allowed her thoughts to drift to the baby, and the excitement she felt at holding her again. She knew instinctively what Sun needed at any given time, and no longer felt awkward in Liu's presence as she nurtured the little girl.

There was no, *do you mind if I do this*, for the baby, or *should we try that?* With Liu's blessing, Paislee was large and in charge with little Sun, and loved every minute of it.

But as she turned the last corner on the ranch road towards the cook house, Paislee thought something looked out of place. It was another car, she realized, and her stomach dropped with a thud, like a brick.

"Oh no," she cried out loud, "no, no NO." Someone was taking the baby away, and she didn't get there in time to stop it. Filled with regret at her late arrival, tears welled up in Paislee's eyes. So much so that she had difficulty seeing a place to park her car.

Breathe, she told herself in the driveway, knowing she couldn't give way to hysteria—Sun would sense her raw nerves and feel insecure. She would never cause grief to the little child. Blowing out and breathing in, Paislee, at last felt able to walk inside and face her worst fears.

"Ling," she exclaimed, seeing Liu's mother standing in the kitchen.

Paislee pushed down a new wave of anxiety as she saw Sun in Ling's arms, wearing a coat and hat. Maybe there was still time to stop her from taking the baby back to the grandmother in Rock Springs.

"Paislee," Liu's mother smiled as she gave a slight bow, then reached in for a more informal embrace. Paislee resisted the urge to grab the baby from her arms.

"I just got back from taking Sun for a walk in her stroller," Ling said to Paislee's relief. "It's not getting warmer for many months, and she needs fresh air."

Paislee smiled and nodded weakly.

Ling watched her closely, frowning slightly at Paislee's obvious distress.

"My daughter tells me you've been coming daily to help with the little orphan," Ling spoke. "I hope it hasn't been an... imposition. You look a little tired, dear."

"*No,* not an imposition at all—it's been a joy," Paislee managed while holding back tears, "pure... joy." Liu also looked at Paislee with concern, and motioned for her to move into the living room and rest on the sofa. Ling walked close behind. Once settled, she placed the baby in Paislee's waiting arms.

"I'm sorry," Paislee attempted, but smiled at the sleeping Sun. "I'm tired, I guess."

"We are all weary. This situation has been hard on everyone," Ling said softly as she and Liu sat in nearby chairs and observed Paislee with the baby. "Sun's grandmother is not well, most days. Her illness is compounded, I think, by concern."

"And my own grandmother is showing signs of a weakened heart," Liu said. Paislee was alarmed by the news, and asked Ling to express her well wishes to Chun for a full recovery.

"You see, we cannot take her in, either." Ling shook her head in sadness. "What is to become of *yīng'ér,* this poor little baby?"

CHAPTER 29

"*D*on't rush your last year, you can't get high school back."

"I don't want to get high school back."

Ridge made a point of staying with Ash until he was sure the boy was in a good place, and that they were okay. He ordered a few deli sandwiches for delivery, and listened to Ash tell him all about the price of subfloors.

He felt pulled to go see Casey, but Ash was his family and his priority. Everything and everyone else would have to wait. This boy, this young man, was growing up right before his very eyes. Ridge knew he didn't have all the time in the world with him.

It also made Ridge quietly wonder how Casey fit into the equation —and if she fit in.

"Still, there's no hurry to conquer the world," Ridge reinforced. "College is waiting for you, and you own your own house. But be a kid for just a little longer, okay?"

Ash broke into a surprised smile at his dad's words, looking younger and more carefree than he had seen in a long time, or maybe ever. It made Ridge feel as though he'd finally said something right.

For too long, life had been telling Ash to act older than he was—to bury his pain of abandonment; to take care of the grandma who could no longer care for him, before he could legally drive a car or manage bills.

The boy needed permission to act his age, Ridge realized.

I need that reminder myself, sometimes.

"Ash," Ridge said, "you don't have to scrabble to succeed, or survive. I'm proud of whatever you do, and I've got you covered, even on days when you have your doubts. So go to a dance, or a game. Go to the movies with friends. Toss around a football, and gaze at the stars. I think there's a horse or two at the ranch who miss riding with you."

His youngest seemed to take it all in, and Ridge hoped he did.

"Tell you what," Ash said, "help me put the lids back on the paint cans, and I'll go ask a friend—Amber—if she wants to take a drive up to Cindy's for an ice cream."

"Deal."

LEAVING ASH'S HOUSE, there was something Ridge very much wanted to do. But first, there was a conversation that needed to take place; one he'd put off for too long.

He gave his son a big bear hug in front of the little houses, and promised to see him back at home later, then made a stop in town for a large bouquet of wildflowers and eucalyptus—her favorites. Grabbing a hot coffee at the drive-through to bolster his resolve, Ridge turned towards West Ranch.

Driving through the massive arches, he allowed himself to gaze at the gorge and the mountains, on fire with bright oranges and yellows from the aspen trees that lined the hillsides. The setting sun created deep shadows that outlined the ridges.

Looking to the very tops, Ridge could see snow that settled on the mountains in the night from the high clouds and cold temps. It wouldn't be long before they got their first blizzard in West Gorge. It would howl and blow and drift for days, coming down from the Pass, near Chuck Barber's ranch. Then the more seasonable sunshine would melt it all again.

"A warning shot, is what that first snowstorm is," Ridge's daddy had told him. "Makes a man batten down the ranch for the real winter —the one that won't melt until spring."

Through the years, Ridge had seen early *warning shot* snowfalls that were barely flurries, and others that buried the town and the roads for days. Not so long ago, Pike and Paislee got caught in such a storm at the old homestead barn. It was enough to cause their love and appreciation for each other to ignite and grow.

That same storm caught Ash in the county jail for a few days, causing him to repent of his wrong actions and turn a more tender heart towards the West family—his family now.

Ridge smiled at the memory of adopting the boy, and the joy it brought both of them. He wished Randi were still alive to know Ash West. She'd be as proud of him as she was her own boys, he just knew.

Turning from the main road and onto a dusty two track, Ridge braced himself for the difficult words he had to say. He slowed the truck until he saw the family cemetery plot ahead, in a clearing of trees.

Parking and exhaling, Ridge took the flower bouquet from the front seat and stepped into the cool air.

The most recent person buried here was Ash's granny. Ridge figured that since Ash was a West, his grandmother should be buried here too. The first to be buried here was his great grandfather, Bluff Fletcher, followed by his grandparents Addie and Pickford West and their babies. After that, Ridge's own parents.

After that...

Ridge cleared his throat and took off his hat, which he held reverently in his hands. Walking over to the marker that read Randi Lynn West, he knelt and lovingly placed the flowers on the grass. Then he sat down and settled in for a spell.

"Darlin'" Ridge said after a time, "we need to talk."

CHAPTER 30

"Welcome, welcome," Paislee bowed slightly as she opened her front door.

Oh, why hadn't she learned to speak Chinese?

Paislee chastised herself, but who had time to learn a new language with a newborn infant demanding every moment of her days and nights? With the Chen's blessing, she took Sun to their house a few days before. But Pike insisted, as gently as possible, that they come to an agreement with the family, so Sun would not be bounced from home to home.

And from heart to heart, Paislee suspected.

"Come in," she said, nervously gesturing to Pike to hang up coats as they guided their guests to their large family room.

The house was new and the rooms big and sunny. They had a large sectional sofa and four oversized chairs upholstered in bright tapestries and brocades.

Paislee liked visual interest, and wouldn't be defined by anyone else's style. But she was glad that one of her chairs had been covered in bright red and yellow floral silk; the Chinese colors for good fortune.

Sun was sleeping soundly in a small portable crib in the family room, and the four Chens, along with Liu, and Sun's great grand-mother, tiptoed over to ooh and aah at the sleeping baby girl. The baby's great grandmother reached down and gently touched her back. Sun stirred slightly, but kept sleeping.

When the older woman turned around to make her way to the sofa, Paislee saw a tear in her eye and had a pang of panic that little Sun was going to be removed from their home—she and Pike had grown so fond of the baby. But then she saw how hard it was for the grandmother to walk. So much so that Zhang, Liu's father, hopped up and took her arm.

The room was full, with Pike playing host and Kat and Willow there for moral support. Willow played quietly with Sun's toys, crawling from one to the next. Liu's own grandparents eagerly got down on the floor to play with the baby, who rewarded them with a smile and laugh of recognition. Willow practically speed crawled to them and gave them both wet sloppy kisses.

"Ah, hello Willow," they exclaimed in happiness.

Again, Paislee's spirits fell. She was sure the Chens would once again push Liu and Colton to take the baby back with them, so she would have Chinese parents. And while Pike thought she was a saint, it wasn't true. She alone knew the jealousy that would flood her heart at family gatherings, watching Liu and Colton with Sun in their arms again.

Paislee knew she'd always wonder why one woman, who wasn't even ready to be a mother, would be handed a beautiful little baby… while another woman, whose arms were empty and aching, was denied that gift.

After serving tea and cookies, the grandmother spoke to Zhang in Chinese.

"Sun's grandmother says you have a beautiful home of great fortune and happiness," Zhang translated for Paislee and Pike, who reached for each other's hands. The grandmother spoke some more.

"She is… ashamed, of her granddaughter's absence, but her heart is full for Sun."

The grandmother nodded and smiled at Paislee, who was now the one near tears.

Paislee bowed to the grandmother, and asked Zhang to express her and Pike's gratitude that she is allowing them to care for little Sun. After that transaction, Paislee turned to Pike, who was going to be the bad cop in the conversation they felt they needed to broach.

"My wife and I would like to continue caring for Sun," he said, "as long as we are favored by her grandmother."

Zhang translated to the grandmother.

"But," Pike said, "to continue doing so, for however long we are favored, we wish to become her legal guardians—so that we can provide Sun with doctor visits, and medical care if she becomes sick."

Zhang again translated, and the grandmother raised her eyebrows in surprise.

"Oi," She said, giving away nothing.

Paislee's stomach was in knots, knowing the grandmother might choose to pack the baby up and take her back to Rock Springs that very day.

Just then, Sun let out a hungry cry. Nearly everyone in the room stood up in response, but it was Paislee who reached the crib first. She cooed at Sun, while quickly changing her diaper. By that time, Pike was at her elbow with a warmed bottle—all while the grandmother watched with great interest.

Holding the dry and hungry baby, tiny fist jammed in her mouth, Paislee carried her over and motioned for the grandmother to sit again, so she could hand her over. Propping a pillow under the grand-mother's arms, Paislee tucked the baby into her waiting hands, and settled the bottle to where Sun could be easily fed, even by aching and arthritic bones.

Like an arrangement for a painting, Paislee stepped back and smiled, admiring her work. She truly wanted what was best for Sun.

The room was silent, but for Willow's babbles and the hungry sucking of Sun as she drank her afternoon bottle. When the bottle became empty and filled with only air, the baby's face crumpled with momentary unhappiness and she let out a cry of distress. Paislee moved to rescue the baby, but stopped herself. She reached out instead for Pike's hand and held it tight.

After a minute, the grandmother looked up and nodded at Paislee, who gladly lifted Sun back into her arms. Placing her over her shoulder, she patted Sun's back while singing gently and gliding around the room.

The baby's audible burp was cause for a loud exclamation of joy from around the room, for everyone but Willow, who began crying at the outburst.

The grandmother turned to Tao, Liu's grandfather, and the two conferred in low tones, in a language only half of the room understood. Ling and Liu cleared the tea into the kitchen, and had their own private conversation.

Paislee looked out the window, trying hard to tune everything out. As a hostess, it was unforgiveable. But as a caregiver to the precious baby in her arms, it was the only way she would get through the next few minutes—and if they took Sun, the next few weeks and months. However long it would take to grieve the baby's loss from their home.

She felt Pike's hand on her back, silently giving her his support. Paislee had fallen even deeper in love with the man these past weeks as he tirelessly assembled a baby swing, a car seat, a high chair... and unpacked endless delivery boxes filled with diapers, formula, blankets and toys. It had been his insistence that they have legal authority to continue caring for Sun, and she would try not to hold it against him when the grandmother refused.

"Pike, Paislee, a moment please." It was Ling, at last.

Paislee turned to look in Pike's eyes, as he gave her half a smile and a nod.

It will be okay, he was telling her; *have courage*. Which was comforting, as it was impossible to read the expression and body language of anybody else in the room.

"Sun's great grandmother would like to thank you for caring so abundantly for the baby when nobody else could," Ling said.

Paislee fought back tears as she was sure they were breaking up with her.

"And, she agrees that for now, you two should be the baby's official guardians. Send your attorneys to her house with the necessary paperwork and she will sign. She has little Sun's birth certificate in her possession, and a letter from the mother relinquishing her rights," Ling translated.

CHAPTER 31

*P*ike held baby Sun in one arm, and his sobbing wife in his other. Hers were tears of happiness—for the time being. But if the baby's great grandmother located a Chinese family willing to take in the baby instead of the young Wests, the tears could turn to inconsolable sorrow overnight.

His wife's heart was so tender, and her love so strong.

Until now, he had been the sole recipient under the roof of the new farmhouse Colton built. But little Sun hadn't divided their love; it had somehow multiplied it. Pike wished he could protect his young wife from pain, as he vowed to when he fell in love with her.

It frightened him now to realize how much was out of his hands and out of his control. He loved Paislee and wanted nothing more than to grant her every heart's desire, which was a baby in her arms. He hadn't realized how deep her longing had been until Sun came into their life.

They had only been married a year, and he thought they might wait a while to start their family. Paisley was everything he never knew he needed in a wife, and every day he vowed to be everything she needed.

At some point in the last year, Pike realize that Paislee had become anxious about not becoming pregnant. It didn't bother him except that it bothered her. She didn't say so, but Pike found dog-eared magazine articles, and heard snippets of conversations between Paislee and her mother, Pepper Andrews.

"I don't know Mama, it just hasn't." Paislee had said.

Pike hadn't known they'd been trying to have a baby. He just thought they were expressing their love for each other as newly married couples did.

When Paislee brought Sun home from Liu's cook house, she said it would just be a few days to help out. Only, Paislee's attachment to Sun was swift and deep. She started out using Willow's baby clothes from Kat, but then packages started to arrive.

Packages had been arriving daily since the day they moved in. Wedding gifts and pantry boxes. Supplemented by the items Paislee chose for their home. An art curator, Paisley also bought paintings and pottery and sculptures online, their four-car garage was quickly filling up with boxes and packing materials to recycle.

It wasn't long before the packages contained baby clothes and toys. Little blankets and diapers and baby food.

Pike was overwhelmed with everything babies seem to need—did he and his brothers have all of the stuff? He couldn't imagine Randi West, his mother, buying cute little outfits for he and his brothers. Especially when they would be out playing in the creek and amongst the sage brush every day, riding horses and roping fence posts, and practicing for the day they'd become cowboys like their daddy.

Pike had grown fond of the baby too, and he would be sad, heartbroken in fact, if she was taken from them. He felt helpless to control the situation, and knew this was one time all the money they had couldn't affect the outcome.

In hindsight, he wished they'd started adoption proceedings in a way that would have protected them from the pain of loving a baby, only to have them removed, but that was naïve; there was always risk involved. Birthing a baby too, had risk. There were no guarantees in life, Pike knew, all too well.

"You just hold on tight, love hard, and do the best you can," his daddy had said when he married Paislee. Pike had forgotten until now, but the words seemed prophetic.

CHAPTER 32

*R*idge knocked on the door of the tri-level while opening it slowly. He must remember to tell her not to leave the door unlocked—if she'd even talk to him.

"Casey?" he called out. He knew from her car that she was here, and probably alone.

The house had been dark except for a few lights flooding the windows. Common sense would have him wait until daylight, but there hadn't been much common sense in their relationship.

"Casey, are you here?"

Ridge could hear scraping sounds, along with sniffles. Followed by a sob. Closing the front door quietly behind him, he stepped towards the sound of her. As he turned a corner towards the lighted living room, something struck him hard on the chest. The size and weight of a baseball, the object was wet and cold.

"Ow... *what* the..." he exclaimed, holding his hands up in surprise.

Casey had lobbed a wadded-up ball of wet wallpaper and glue that she'd scraped off. It felt like a rock. Shocked, Ridge looked up again in time to see another wad flying towards him. This one struck him on the shoulder as he took a step backwards.

"Casey, I..." he held his hands up and walked towards her.

"Get out!" Casey yelled at him while forming another ball. Her face was blotchy from crying, and her anger was red hot.

"You tried to trick me, Casey, but you were wrong." Ridge was a little angry too as he closed the distance between them.

"I was right, you can't be trusted," she yelled in a hoarse voice. "Leave, now!"

"No. I came for something," Ridge told her, walking carefully towards her as if she was a wild mustang, "and I'm not leaving without it."

Casey threw another wad, but they were standing too close and it didn't have much impact. She opened her mouth to yell, but nothing came out.

"I thought you were my friend." She spoke hoarsely, through chokes and tears.

"I am," he said in a whisper, near tears himself. "The Shires... it wasn't how it looked."

Oh, what had he done?

She shook her head miserably, and her shoulders sagged in defeat. The anger in her eyes had turned to sadness, and her lips trembled. Ridge feared she might faint or fall. He closed the last few inches between them and let his hands rest on her still tense and angry body.

Her back was hard and rigid, but he encircled her waist by tiny increments until she exhaled some of the anger. As she trembled, he leaned closer, whispering her name into her silky hair.

"Casey," his low voice rumbled. "Oh, *Casey.*"

"*What* Ridge," she whispered. "What did you come for?"

Pulling her close to his own chest and heart, he tilted his head and softly kissed her neck, once, twice, three times. He brushed his lips up and along her jawline, whispering her name.

Her breathing was soft but jagged, as through tears. Eyes closed and lips slightly parted, she turned her face up towards his.

"Uh uh," he shook his head. He wasn't finished exploring the soft skin of her neck.

When Casey opened her eyes, he brought his hand up and ran a thumb along her cheek and jaw, noting the surprise of her gaze.

"This," he whispered to her. "I came for this. I came for you."

At last, the corner of Ridge's mouth curved into a partial smile and he brought his lips to hers, tenderly, but stubbornly—he wouldn't back away unless she told him to stop.

For a moment, she remained like a rag doll in his arms. Then her hands rested on his forearms; slowly, they traveled up, caressing every bone and muscle along the way. When her hands finally reached his shoulders, she wrapped herself around him and pulled him tight, melting into his body.

Ridge kissed her harder, and then softer again. Over and over.

"I'm sorry Casey girl, I'm sorry," Ridge said, pulling away just a little bit. Looking into her eyes, he saw a glimmer of trust, and silently vowed to never jeopardize that again.

CHAPTER 33

"I thought you hated me," Casey said softly.

They were sitting on the shag carpet of the tri-level, leaning against the grass cloth wallpaper in the living room and holding hands.

"There's nothing about you to hate," Ridge said just as softly as he squeezed Casey's hand. "I'm the one that's not looking too good these days."

He smiled over at her.

"That's not completely true," she laughed a little. "You've been looking too good. That's my problem. I haven't been able to keep my mind on business."

"Well I'm staying out of your business from now on. Hanging up my real estate hat, and going back to ranching, where I belong," Ridge said. "You can list all my properties for me."

Casey sat up straighter and looked at him, to see if he was telling the truth.

"No, I mean it," he said. "I just wanted to be close to Ash. And then to you—but all I managed to do was push you both away, and make a fool of myself."

"You're being too hard on yourself," she said. "You aren't a foolish man, Ridge. You're passionate and devoted—and loyal. My dad had those qualities."

"Had?" He asked her.

Casey looked over at Ridge with a sad smile. "I miss him terribly, and mother too. He and I worked together, you see, so our bond was strong. I promised him I'd find a man with his good qualities, but I missed the mark."

"There was… someone else?" Ridge knew so little about Casey.

She nodded distractedly.

"Do you have a dog, Ridge?" Casey looked over and asked with a smile.

Ridge reeled at her change in topic.

"Yeah… yes, we have always had dogs at the ranch."

"You know how we tend to humanize pets, interjecting human qualities like warmth, and loyalty? But then sometimes… sometimes it acts out on pure instinct, and you realize it was just a dog all along. *Just a dog.*"

Ah, she wasn't talking about dogs. Ridge stayed quiet. He wanted to get his hands on that dog, though.

"But you, Ridge West," Casey rolled her head back towards him, and seemed to be in the present, "you are a gentleman. Daddy would have liked you."

"How you can say that, the way I've acted."

"What did you do that was so terrible? You gave Miss Emily a bonus at the end of her hard-scrabble life; you lined a few other well-deserved pockets along the way; and you kept me on my professional toes—I've had the best year ever since running from… since moving to town."

"You almost make me sound *nice,*" he said in a low rumble, with a mischievous smile. "You're going to ruin my bad boy reputation."

"Well, there was a little mischief in those kisses."

Ridge shifted with pleasure at the memory. Casey Parks was the first woman he'd kissed since marrying Randi Lynn as a young man. He thought it would feel strange and wrong. But Casey's kisses were warm and wonderful; both new and familiar—not strange at all.

"Does that mean you'd go out with me, on a date?" Even though they were holding hands, Ridge felt nervous asking.

Casey opened her mouth to accept, he thought, when her phone rang. Immediately, Ridge could see the fear in her eyes again as she looked at the screen to silence the ring.

It was that dog calling, Ridge suspected.

He only hoped its bark was worse than its bite.

CHAPTER 34

$\mathcal{P}$aislee's stomach tightened up in a ball when she saw Liu standing at her door. Through the leaded transom window, she could see that Liu was holding a pot of blooming Mums.

Does Liu want the baby back?

Does she think she'll trade cheap flowers for Sun?

Trying to breathe deeply before opening the door, Paislee braced herself for the worst.

"Liu," she said in a theatrical whisper. "Come in. I just put the baby upstairs for a nap."

Liu smiled a tired smile and set the flowers on the porch.

"These are for your garden, Paislee," she said. "If you plant them before the snow, they should come back in the spring."

Paislee thanked her, and then walked towards the kitchen to make tea, expecting Liu to follow her. She hadn't said much, as she didn't trust her voice. She would let Liu do the talking.

"Your house is beautiful," Liu said, looking at the walls of artwork and colorful furnishings. There were a few expensive looking antiques, no doubt from the Andrews family home.

"Yours will be too," Paislee managed. "Colton is a master builder, and his craftsmanship is as pretty as I've ever seen."

Liu smiled in gratitude at the kind words.

"Join me at the table, won't you?" Paislee carried a tray to the kitchen table overlooking the back yard, and the painting studio and guesthouse.

"I'm sorry to surprise you," Liu said, "but I had to come talk to you while I had the courage."

Oh no... courage! Paislee thought in despair. *This sounds bad.*

Paislee willed herself not to cry, but her eyes pooled with un-spilled tears.

"The courage... for what?" Paislee choked out.

"The courage... to walk away from the baby, Paislee," Liu managed. "To ask you and Pike to consider adopting her as your own child."

Paislee couldn't help but gasp in surprise, and she nearly dropped the antique china cup that she held in her shaking hand.

"Don't tease me about this, Liu," Paislee whispered through tears, now flowing freely.

"I would not do that," Liu said. She reached over and took Paislee's hand.

"No," Paislee said, more confidently than before, "of course not."

Liu went on to explain that she was raised on more than a little guilt, and sense of obligation. But that, thanks to Colton, she is learning to accept that not all expectations are hers to carry. If push came to shove, she said, she and Colton would step up and take in Sun, for the baby's welfare. But after seeing her with Paislee and Pike, they realized that some *opportunities*, for she would never consider Sun a burden, are others' blessings.

"I would have robbed you of the blessing, just to assuage my own guilt. But Sun is obviously meant to be in your arms," Liu said with a slight bow. "*Xièxiè nǐ,* thank you for caring for her, and loving her as you do, with your whole heart."

Paislee couldn't believe her ears.

"I would have loved her if there was no one else," Liu continued, "but it would have been half-hearted. At first anyway, while I would pray for love to grow. You already love her."

"I do love her," Paislee said. "From the moment you put her in my arms, she was my own flesh and blood—and heart. That's why I couldn't stay away. But I want you to be sure, Liu. It's not too late to change your mind, if you feel that's for the best."

Liu stared at Paislee and considered her words. The pull to please her mother was strong, but in her heart, she knew the right thing to do.

"I'll do everything in my power to support Sun's right to be with you and Pike," Liu said. "I'll be a character witness, babysitter, or whatever you need Auntie Liu to be."

CHAPTER 35

"*I*t's a little cold for a picnic."

Ridge and Casey were driving into the mountains with a thermos of hot coffee, and roast beef sandwiches Liu made up earlier that day, at his request. And of course, Liu couldn't assemble a picnic for anyone in the family without her famous spring rolls, and her most recent *triumph*—oatmeal raisin cookies.

Liu couldn't forget, it seemed, the praise Ridge lavished on her for the chocolate cake she made on his birthday, and tried to replicate that approval every chance she had.

"The day started out warmer," Ridge agreed with a laugh.

He looked up towards the Pass, and the direction of Chuck Barber's ranch. That's where the snow would be the heaviest when it landed later—as predicted by the weather service. Ridge wondered if Casey knew about the listing, but didn't want to talk "shop" with her on their first date.

"We'll stay as long or as little as we want. I've got a blanket to sit on, and a wool throw for our legs."

"Just one wool throw—to share?" Casey had a seductive tease in her voice that sent shock waves up and down Ridge's spine.

Now that they'd tasted their first kisses, Ridge was on high alert navigating the newness of their relationship. He didn't want to move too fast if they were not meant to be. If Ash was right, someone broke Casey's heart, and he wasn't about to cause her more pain.

But they weren't kids, and things could move pretty fast. It was all the excitement of driving a Lamborghini, with one cautious foot on the brake.

"I'll keep you warm," he said with a sly smile as he slowed to find a place to park, with one hand on the wheel and one hand holding Casey's. They were each lost in the view out the window, and their own thoughts.

This wasn't the time to think about Randi, but Ridge remembered how effortless their early love had been. From the moment they set eyes on each other, there was no doubt they would marry and build a life together. Their first days were filled with red-hot passion and energy. Completely smitten with each other, they jumped right over the slow wooing of dating, diving head first into married life.

He was older now—much older. With complications, entanglements, and the feelings of others to consider. His brief conversation with Ash revealed that.

Casey had stuff of her own. She had *trust issues,* Ash said in anger when he thought Ridge was being clumsy with her feelings. He wouldn't have to wait much longer though. When he invited her, she asked if he wouldn't mind hearing her story, and why she left Phoenix.

Carrying the basket and blankets, Casey carried the thermos and mugs. Ridge reached over for her hand again as they gently hiked along the West River foot path. They'd find a spot next to large boulders that would block the chill wind, he told her. Promising the next date would be indoors.

"This is a nice spot," Casey pointed to a clearing, and Ridge stopped to spread a blanket on the pine-needle ground. As he unpacked their lunch and poured the coffee, Casey covered their legs with the throw.

"Get a little closer," he said, enjoying the feel of her. She tucked her body against his at every contact point she could—seeking the warmth she'd been missing.

CHAPTER 36

"Once upon a time," Casey said after taking a few bites of her sandwich, "I had nine agents working for me, and a beautiful office located in a historic downtown brick building. There was a donut shop on the corner, and we got a lot of foot traffic and referral business."

Casey smiled at the memory.

"My daddy built the company, and I took over before he..." she said, inferring rather than speaking the event of his passing. It was still too painful.

"Derek Vance joined as a junior-level agent." Casey laughed, but not a joyful laugh. It was filled with regret and pain. "He really wasn't very good, but he was charming, and disarming. Clients loved him; *women* loved him. The wives, widows, and girlfriends—they adored him, and gave us their business. One listing after another. He claimed I was the only one he looked at, and I was gullible, I suppose."

Casey stopped talking, and swallowed hard. Some words were harder to say than others.

"I guess he used a little charm on me, because he convinced me that we were partners. It only seemed fair that we should run the company like partners, and have the money in a joint account."

How had he done that?

Casey could not remember, but their early days were a blur.

"All too late, I began to suspect I wasn't the only one he had eyes for," Casey admitted. "When the market got soft a few years ago, he panicked and ran. But it wasn't enough to take his money, he wanted mine too. And then he wanted everyone else's. I'm embarrassed to tell you how easy I made it for him to rob the company blind."

Casey looked over and watched Ridge's face for his reaction.

"Okay," Ridge said, "but you were the victim. What's he holding over you now?"

"He must figure that a man like you wouldn't want to associate with my past failings. You see, when Derek was done destroying my business, he set about ruining my good name to cover his tracks."

Casey spilled more of the story to Ridge. She'd carried it alone far too long. Ridge reached over and took Casey's hand, and she allowed it.

"Based on a tip from Derek, and the testimony of an angry agent, a local paper reported on the Parks Realty 'scandal' and how I was at the heart of it. That's when I left town."

Jaw open, Ridge was incredulous at the revelation.

"Why didn't you go after him?" Ridge's question was fair.

Casey shrugged. "I had no money, no family or friends, and no fight left in me," she said. "I used my own funds to pay the commissions of my agents—as much as possible, anyway. Derek didn't just steal from me; he took from them too. I paid what I could, and tried to start over in Phoenix. But my name was ruined. Nobody trusted me. Not sellers, or buyers, or agents... I dissolved the company and left."

But that's not the whole truth, tell him.

"Also," Casey sighed, "I was humiliated. I thought he and I... that *we*... I'd put all my apples in one basket, named Derek Vance. I just felt so ashamed, and stupid. I fell for the oldest trick in the book, and I thought I was smarter."

Choosing his words, Ridge spoke carefully.

"Let me get this straight," he said. "You were robbed, cheated, embarrassed… and then made to look like the guilty party?"

Casey shrugged and nodded. "It was just easier to move and start over, than starting over alone in a town with a bad reputation," she said.

There was silence between them as Ridge listened patiently.

"The worst part is… though I'm ashamed to say my feelings out loud… is that I gave that man my youth, and so the very best years of my life," she said with sadness.

Ridge looked over in surprise at his beautiful date. Her skin was dewy, and flushed from their hike. Her eyes held sparkles and facets of light, like geodes. Casey's hair waved with silky, unruly curls that shined with silvery highlights left over from the summer sun.

She was a stunner, more than she knew.

"That's where I have to object," Ridge said, to her surprise. "I'd be willing to bet that the best years of your life are still ahead."

Looking sad and defeated, Casey shrugged and took a bite of her sandwich.

"You see, Casey, you gave him *Phoenix* years," Ridge said with a smile.

"Phoenix… years?"

Wrapping her hands around her coffee mug for warmth, Casey looked over.

"Let me tell you about Wyoming years," Ridge went on, leaning back and gazing at the gorge. "The beauty of Wyoming can shave years off a life," he said.

"Is that so?" Casey smiled, wanting it to be true.

"Yep, time stands still here."

"I'd like to believe you," she laughed.

"I guarantee, you look younger now than when you came to town, looking like a fussy librarian with your hair in a tight bun."

She laughed again at his apt description.

"Every time you gaze at the water running through the gorge, or smile up at the aspen trees, all yellow in the hazy autumn sun, you turn back time just a little."

Ridge reached over and tucked a wayward curl behind Casey's ear.

You just keep smiling, Casey Parks, with those beautiful lips parted in wonder.

"Well it's true in your case," Casey said as she looked into his crystal-clear eyes. "The way you walk, you could pass for a teenager—like you owned the world and everything in it."

Ridge started to lean over to kiss the woman who made him feel like a teenager, when a cold gust of wind blew down from the mountains and chilled them to the bone.

"Whoa, we'd better get out of the cold," Casey said, and they hurriedly stood to go. Gathering the blankets and thermos, she jogged towards the truck. When they were within eyesight of it, Ridge ran up close behind her and gave her a playful slap on the bottom.

"I'll beat you there," he said, and dashed ahead.

"You... you did *not* just do that, Ridge West," she slowed her pace and sputtered into the cold wind, insulted and aghast; unsure whether to laugh or yell.

"Oh, I did," he said with such unabashed unrepentance, that she could only shake her head as he held the door for her, waiting with his outstretched hand. "In case I haven't mentioned it, you're a fine one, Casey Parks. Now let's go."

"Hmm," Casey said before accepting his hand to step into the truck, while trying to suppress a smile, "I think Wyoming took a few too many years off of you."

She leaned up and kissed his cold face, as the first snowflakes of the season teased the air.

CHAPTER 37

"*I* ruined you in Phoenix, and I can ruin you in that little town you're in," the ominous voice said over the phone. Casey had been brewing a mug of hot tea at home when she saw his name on her caller ID.

Knowing she couldn't avoid Derek forever, she pressed the button to answer, but didn't speak. Apparently, he had no shortage of things to say and got right to it.

"There's a newspaper in West Gorge just dying to print some juicy gossip, especially after months of boring old articles about the price of beef, and the dangers of oak wilt."

Casey cringed at his words—he really did know where she lived now.

"My sources tell me you're doing well and dating a rich cowboy. Maybe he'd be interested to find out who you really are."

Sources?

"He already knows," Casey spoke at last.

"His family doesn't know though, do they?" he asked, menacingly. "Not the ones who matter. *They* don't know who you are, do they Cassidy—or should I say, *Casey?*"

Again, Casey cringed just thinking of the Phoenix article, accusing her of mismanaging funds, stiffing her employees, and running her father's business into the ground. It was all true, even if it wasn't her doing. Her crime was trusting the wrong man, but that didn't make a good headline.

It was old news.

Casey thought back to the Phoenix article and the photo they printed; the one she saw in her nightmares, and tried hard to forget.

Unbeknownst, a photographer with a long lens captured her loading boxes into her car; behind her, the CLOSED sign was taped on the real estate agency window. With her dour expression and sunglasses, she certainly did look guilty, and very much like someone trying to skip town. If the West Gorge newspaper reprinted that picture, everyone would quickly jump to their own conclusions and life would become an uphill battle.

And then, how could Ridge possibly be proud to introduce her to the West family?

Casey knew the value of a good reputation, which Ridge earned and deserved. His family would insist any woman dating their patriarch have good standing in the community—like a Kindergarten teacher, or church choir director.

He deserved better.

If she was out of the picture, Casey thought, Ridge would be free to fall in love with someone else. A sweet widow, maybe. A woman whose heartbreak wasn't as unsavory as hers. A woman who didn't have dirty laundry hanging out for the world to see.

No, there was only one thing to do. She had to distance herself from Ridge, and protect him from the trouble Derek was fully prepared to stir up.

"I know you, Cassidy Casey Parks, and I can see your gears turning, even over the phone." Derek sounded mean, like a dangerous stranger. Casey's stomach hurt just listening to him, and couldn't believe she'd ever loved and trusted him.

"You go ahead and mull this over," he continued, "because I know you'll make the right decision. You always do."

Not always, she thought.

"Don't take too long. I need to see some Benjamins showing up in my account. And when I do, your tragic downfall will stay our little secret."

But for how long? Would he keep coming back, over and over again—would she never be able to love without the fear of revealing her past?

Casey didn't wait for Derek to say another word. She couldn't bear it. She hung up on him without ceremony, and took her now-cold tea to her sofa. It was clear Derek wasn't going to let her go—but would Ridge?

She would never forget the way he'd entered the tri-level the other night, and took her in his arms. It was nothing short of heroic. She had been fighting mad, and throwing hard balls of wet wallpaper at him like stones. But he took her in his arms and kissed her, like she'd never been kissed in her life.

This was not a man who would take her rejection lying down.

CHAPTER 38

"*Y*ou are my sunshine, my only sunshine."

Ridge couldn't remember the last time he tried to sing, and suddenly pitied anyone who'd ever sat in front of him at church—but he couldn't stop himself this morning. His pitch wasn't perfect, but Willow didn't care as he danced and twirled her around the kitchen.

Socks were perfect, he realized happily, for effortlessly spinning your dance partner on the smooth tile floors of the ranch.

"You make me happy when skies are gray," he sang to the laughing baby before setting her back down amidst her toys.

"Well someone's in a good mood," Kat said, entering the kitchen. She was dressed in a rust-colored wool suit and cream blouse, meaning she would be leaving for the hospital.

"Who's watching the baby today?" Ridge asked, hoping to divert Kat's keen attention. She eyed him suspiciously, but didn't probe any further.

"Jackie," Kat said at last. "And I'm sure she'll bring you a few ribs."

"Nice," he said.

Jackie was the hospital nurse who set Kat up on a blind date with Gunnar a few years before, when she moved to the town. Recently,

Jackie wanted to pull back from the medical field to help her husband run his flourishing BBQ restaurant. They were so busy they were considering a second location, and mass producing their wildly popular sauce. Gunnar offered to underwrite the venture.

When Kat offered Jackie a flexible nannying job, for much more than she made as a nurse, Jackie jumped at the opportunity. And she never came empty handed. The West family frequently discovered a fresh supply of BBQ sauce in their pantry, and food in their fridge—including ribs, slaw, beans, and Ridge's personal favorite, succulent and tangy *burnt ends*.

"What are your plans for the day?" Kat picked up Willow and set her in a high chair for breakfast of scrambled eggs, banana slices, and cut up squares of toast. The baby waved her hands excitedly at the feast and dove in with her pudgy fists.

"Oh..." Ridge thought for a minute before answering.

Taking a beautiful woman to lunch, maybe.

Kissing said woman thoroughly on the lips, perhaps.

"I guess the bungalow next to Ash needs some attention," he finally said, while thinking, *Casey's slender neck, and trim, flannel-covered waistline needs some attention, too.*

As if she could read his thoughts, Kat's eyes narrowed with suspicion.

"If you ask me..." she started to say, when the front doorbell rang. Jackie, no doubt, here to bring the ribs and save his bacon. After a quick greeting, he ducked back over to his side of the house, and far away from eagle-eye Kat West.

Ridge just wasn't ready to disclose his new interest—a *mutual* interest, he marveled—in the lovely Casey Parks. He'd never broached the subject of dating with his sons, and didn't know how they'd feel. They could take the news poorly, and Ridge wouldn't blame them.

He was just as stunned.

It never crossed Ridge's mind that he might be interested in love after losing his wife. A few women from town let it be known that they were definitely interested in him, though, bringing potato chip-covered casseroles long past the acceptable timeframe after his loss.

And on Sundays, Ridge often had to duck out the church's side door to avoid a certain group of widows. This gang liked to corner him in the fellowship hall—with motives, he suspected, that were a little more *Song of Solomon* than he was prepared for.

The men in town were just as bad. Like a bunch of gossipy hens, they were constantly trying to set him up with their widowed sister, or spinster cousin. Even Nels Scott, his fishing buddy, said his wife Marta talked of putting Ridge's love life on the town prayer chain.

"I told her flat out 'no way'," Nels said, making Ridge thankful. "I said, *Mart*, if God wanted Ridge to find love again, He'd drop a woman in his lap."

Ridge smiled at the story. He didn't mention to Nels the beautiful woman who had fallen out of a maple tree a few weeks ago, right onto his lap—and onto his chest, and arms, and legs. He was still sore from that fall, but maybe God wanted him to remember it, for a long, long time.

CHAPTER 39

"Ready for tummy time?"

Paislee carried Sun from the kitchen to the family room to play. Sun was especially crabby and in need of distractions.

The baby looked flushed, and rubbed her face clumsily with closed fists while protesting loudly.

"Are you getting a tooth? Can I take a peek?"

Paislee rubbed her finger along the baby's gum line, but didn't feel anything pushing through. She had hoped Sun would play for a while, and then maybe settle down for a long afternoon nap. Paislee was feeling tired herself, so it was very much wishful thinking.

Looking longingly out the window towards Pike's studio, Paislee gasped a little at the snow coming down. She tried to smile at the memory of the blizzard that trapped them both in the ancient settler's barn a year before, where they quickly fell in love—but smiling was just too much effort at the moment.

Pike, she knew, was in the throes of a new oil painting in his studio. She wished he'd come into the house and spell her, but didn't want to disturb him. She should be able to handle one fussy baby, but her eyelids felt so heavy.

"Here we go." She positioned Sun on her stomach upon a thick and colorful play pad, with bright chewy toys and soft stuffed dolls to grab onto.

Standing up, Paislee felt a little dizzy and quickly sat down on the sofa near the baby. A few short weeks ago, she would have stretched out and pulled a throw over her legs for a rest. But no more; her schedule was at the mercy of little Sun day and night.

Paislee fought to keep her eyes open as Sun gave out a howl of unhappiness. The baby grabbed a handful of the quilt in her tiny hands, and squished her face into it while squirming and fretting.

"There there, little one." Paislee reached down and patted her back. Maybe if she fell asleep, she could just cover her up instead of disturbing her by moving her to the crib. But contrary to settling in, the baby's howls got louder and more pronounced. And shockingly, her cheeks felt even warmer to the touch than before.

Suddenly alert, Paislee picked her up and walked her to the kitchen to find the first aid kit.

Paislee recently gave Pike a gentle ribbing at the packages *he* had started ordering. While she had daily deliveries of pink outfits, little leather shoes, and bitty jackets, Pike's boxes contained emergency supplies, childproof locks, and a new car seat that Paislee joked was bulletproof, shatterproof, and as water resistant as any of Pike's fancy diving watches.

Searching with one hand for a thermometer, Sun's cries started taking on an earnestness Paislee had never heard before, and she felt overwhelmed. Walking over to the wall, she pressed the intercom button they had Colton install for communication between the house and the painting studio.

"Pike, sorry, but I need you. *Quick.*"

Mere seconds later, Pike rushed into the kitchen, wiping paint off his hands and pausing to shake a deep layer of snow onto the rug by the door. He would later tell the emergency room doctor that Paislee looked like she was about to topple over, and Sun was flushed and in a great deal of distress.

"Here, sit down," he said to his wife as he took the baby.

"I think… she has… a fever," Paislee managed to say, while closing her eyes.

Paislee would later tell the doctor she had no memory of Pike rushing the baby to the car where he strapped her into her seat—howling and crying. Or lifting Paislee in his arms and carrying her to the car, where he did the same.

He would have called the emergency phone number, he told his family, but knew he could get help faster on his own by driving. Especially with the snow coming down.

With Sun crying so hard she was practically hyperventilating, and Paislee passed out in the back seat, Pike drove carefully on the snowy roads, willing himself not to speed. When he trusted his voice, he commanded his phone.

"Call Kat."

CHAPTER 40

A relative newcomer to the family, nobody could mobilize the troops quite like Kat. As a physician, she was calm under pressure. As a mother, she knew how to prioritize emergency responses, and how to cascade directives. And as a West, she knew how to kick butt and take names.

Though Kat worked largely from her home office these days, she happened to be at the hospital when Pike said he was on his way to the emergency entrance. Paislee was practically unresponsive, he told her. He didn't have to say much about the baby—Kat could hear her shrieking in the background.

After putting the ER team on alert to have a gurney for Paislee and a rolling bassinet for Sun, she made her next calls.

Yes, her sitter at the house, Jackie, said she could stay at the ranch for as long as needed.

Yes, Gunnar would make his way from the ranch to the hospital, after first calling Ash and Ridge to do the same. The two were likely in town, at their bungalows.

Yes, Colton would bring Liu to the hospital. He would ask Liu to call her family to let them know the baby was ill.

"Tell them she's in good hands," Kat told Colton, "and not to venture out in this weather."

As she made her way through the corridors to the ER entrance, she spoke with Josh Quell, second in command for the Infectious Disease Department, and apprised him of the situation. Then she passed Marta in the gift shop and gave her a wave, promising to stop back when she could to catch up.

By the time she got to the ER door, Pike's car was pulling into the covered entryway.

"Let's go," someone on the ER team said, and no fewer than five people went outside to shepherd Paislee and the baby inside.

A crying Sun went off towards the pediatric ER ward, while Paislee went the other direction into triage. Kat watched while Pike's head bobbed back and forth like he was watching a tennis game—until he finally looked helplessly at Kat.

"Hey cowboy," she said firmly, "I want you to follow your wife, and I'm going to follow the baby. If they have questions about Sun, they'll come and find you. Or I will."

Pike opened his mouth to protest, but Kat placed her hands reassuringly on his arms.

"You've got this, Pike," Kat said, nodding her head up and down until Pike's breathing steadied, and he did the same. "Now," she said, "give the valet your car keys."

Before she went to check on Sun, Kat stopped at the admissions desk and asked them to keep an eye out for various and assorted Wests, who would be wandering in all wild and wide-eyed, "looking like they're trying to stop a bank robbery," she said. "Direct them all to the private family waiting area."

The VIP room held unpleasant memories, she knew, from Randi's long bout with cancer. It also held happy memories, of when the family gathered to await Willow's birth. Today, it would be the best location for the family to have privacy. A perk of donating the hospital.

The Wests wouldn't want special treatment, but Kat knew they were a big, loud bunch. She also knew it wouldn't be long before Jackie would have dinner sent to the family, compliments of Red's Rib Shack.

It would be cruel and unusual punishment for non-family members to be teased by the fine aromas of Red's succulent cooking.

CHAPTER 41

"*I*'m sorry, Ridge, I need you to leave," Casey said sadly. "Kissing, dating, you and me... it was all a mistake. We can't be together."

This was not the conversation he expected when he showed up at her apartment bearing flowers, chocolates, and hot coffees. He wanted to go for a drive in the mountains, "without hiking in the cold this time," he said, expecting at least a smile.

He told her snow was coming, but thought they could get out for an hour before it hit in earnest. He'd surely be stuck at the ranch for a few days, with Casey alone at her place.

"You can't be with me today, you mean?"

"Not ever," she said, not wanting to play games. "I can never be with you Ridge."

Ridge's brow furrowed deeply as he tried to make sense of what she was saying. Their kisses had been the real deal, no denying that. And he knew the attraction between them was real. So what then?

Casey hung her head and sniffled quietly.

"*He* called, didn't he?" Ridge asked, but already knew the answer.

That dirty old dog.

She turned away and walked to the window, which only

confirmed his theory. She got a call from Phoenix again... but, she told Ridge everything. Was she holding something back?

"He's got nothing on you, Casey girl. You said so yourself."

Casey nodded as she turned to face him.

"Derek made me realize one thing, Ridge. Whether or not I pay him, the story is going to come out sometime, and it won't look good. People will jump to their own conclusions, and you'll be dragged down with me. I couldn't bear it."

"Wait," Ridge said, trying to take her hand. She pulled away. "You're protecting *me*?"

She looked up and nodded once.

"But I'm already the town bad boy, didn't you know that?"

Casey was not budging in her resolve, he could tell. She would not joke or be cajoled.

"Look, Casey, I'll tell your story and clear things up. Folks will understand."

"No they won't, Ridge," she hissed and shouted in pain and anger. "There are photos, and headlines, and hurtful quotes from my former employees. It looks really bad, and it is bad. *I'm* bad for you."

She was pacing the room, crying tears of frustration as she spoke.

"Your wife," Casey continued, "she was a saint, Ridge. When your kids see the news stories from Phoenix, and they will, they'll be ashamed to have me in your life. I know it. I've seen it for myself."

"It won't happen, Casey."

"Trust me, the paper will dig up the story... or someone will search my name when we go public. They'll see it online. Maybe they already have."

"*What story*—that you were treated badly? I dare them to try and drag your name down." Ridge was getting angry, but so was Casey.

"What are you going to do, buy the paper, Ridge? Same way you bought up those houses that should have been on the fair market? You can't go around buying everything you want—you can't buy my good name or a halo to go over my head. I made mistakes, and trusted the wrong man. I was foolish, and a lot of people were hurt. My employees had to take a fraction of their pay..."

"Which you gave them from your own money."

"Who better? I'm the idiot who allowed it. I deserved what I got."

"I don't agree. But even if you did deserve it, you've paid your dues Casey. Let it go, and let yourself be happy."

"Your family would never allow it, nor should they," she said, quieter than in the heat of anger, "Randi's name is everywhere in town, associated with good works and kind deeds. I just can't compete with her, Ridge."

With her head in her hands, she looked so defeated and helpless.

"I'm not her."

"Well, I'm not him, Casey," Ridge cried out. "I'm not going to abandon you, or hurt you. And you may be afraid of him, but I'm not."

Casey smiled but it only looked sad.

"You're a cowboy, and you want to go guns blazing—find the bad guy and root him out. But I don't need to be rescued. Not now or ever. I've made it on my own, and I can do it again and again if I need to. There's no shortage of towns across this country where I can start over."

"Aren't you tired of…" Ridge was going to finish his sentence with "on your own" when he heard multiple dings and buzzing on his phone. Someone was trying to get him; maybe several someone's, from the sound of it.

Looking down, he could see texts from Ash, Gunnar, and also Pike.

"Somethings wrong, give me a minute," he said to Casey, then, "looks like I have to go to the hospital for a family emergency. Will you *please* come with me?"

Casey had so much longing and loneliness in her eyes, but shook her head.

"You go, Ridge. They need you."

But I need you! He desperately wanted to say.

"We're not done with this conversation, Casey Parks," he said as he buttoned his coat.

CHAPTER 42

"*D*id anyone reach Dad?"

Gunnar asked Ash and Colton, who were pacing the floor of the private waiting room. Pike was sitting in a corner chair, talking to Liu about the baby. Paislee and Sun were stable, but he had no further news about what was making them sick.

"Thought Dad might be with you, Ash," Gunnar said.

"I think he's out on a date with Casey Parks," Ash replied, just as casually as if it were an everyday occurrence. The other brothers looked up sharply.

"A *date*—are you sure?" Gunnar sounded shocked.

"Who's Casey Parks?" Pike lifted his head from the corner and chimed in.

"A date in the afternoon?" Colton sounded less shocked, and a little amused.

"Well, Dad is past 60," Ash said innocently. "Maybe he's not comfortable driving at night."

The three brothers exchanged a look and Colton choked back a laugh—highly inappropriate, considering the circumstances.

"You'd better keep *that* speculation to yourself," Colton told Ash with a smile, ruffling the top of the boy's head the way he used to when Ash first came to the ranch. Although with each passing year, he was forced to reach higher and higher.

Ash smiled back good-naturedly. He pretended to be bothered, but secretly enjoyed the attentions of his older brothers, now busy being husbands and in Gunnar's case, fathers. He'd spent so much of his life with just his Granny. And while he missed her, he thanked God every day for the Wests, and the way they took him into their fold, just like they'd always known him.

"I suppose it must be strange for you to think of Dad dating," Ash carefully said to his brothers. "I never knew your mama, and I know you all miss her. I wish I'd known her. But Casey is nice and smart, and really pretty. I think you'd like her."

Gunnar's smile dimmed just a bit as the full meaning of Ash's words sunk in.

"I'll take your word on that, Ash," Gunnar said, reaching out to give Ash's shoulder a squeeze. Gunnar's voice was thick, like he had something caught in his throat, Ash thought.

Gunnar walked to the window and gazed outside at the storm. He was glad Kat was under the same roof, and wished Willow was here too, but knew she was better off at the ranch, with the trusted Jackie. A quick phone call confirmed that all was well. Rowdy and Gray were nearby and would help if needed.

"I'm just going to assume I'm spending the night at the ranch," she told her old friend. "Don't try to make it home until the roads are clear and safe—we're fine."

He wished Kat was with him in the waiting room, but knew she was glued to baby Sun, as she should be. As much as the pediatric doctors would allow her to be. He also knew Kat would be highly tuned to Ash's insecurities, seeing as she herself had been abandoned by her father at a young age.

He wanted to fold inward a little, and just *feel* the feelings and fear of change, but Kat would expect him to lead the family, and set a tone that would put Ash at ease.

What would Kat do?

Gunnar thought about it for a minute and broke into a grin,

remembering how they fell in love during the quarantine a few years before. Ash was here too. Gunnar didn't like Kat at first, and started calling her "sheriff," on account of her take-charge ways, a term of endearment he still used. In the same spirit, she *deputized* Gunnar to keep Ash out of trouble.

Kat would deputize him again if she were here.

"Ash," Gunnar turned and walked towards the boy. "It might be strange for you to see him dating too—he's not just our dad, he's yours. Are you okay with this, and where it might lead?"

Ash seemed to consider Gunnar's words.

"You mean, if they get married?"

Gunnar's head started spinning at hearing the thought spoken out loud. He sat down and tried to swallow the panic rising up in his throat. Finally, he nodded.

"You don't think he'd forget about me, do you Gunnar?"

Oh man, Gunnar felt so inadequate as he looked into the frightened eyes of Ash—seeing the same fear that was probably in his own eyes. Would Ridge forget about their family—and their mother?

"No!" Gunnar said emphatically, meaning it.

"No. The West gang is growing like crazy, but love doesn't divide —it multiplies." He put his hand on Ash's shoulder once again. "We will always look out for each other, and put each other's interests at the heart of what we do. That's who we are. That's who Dad is."

Ash nodded and looked more at peace. Gunnar smiled at the boy, thinking of how much he'd grown up since coming to West Ranch, and how good it was that Ash could verbalize his worries, instead of acting out.

Kat would be proud of him—of them all.

CHAPTER 43

I'm not her.
 I'm not him!
Shadows of his argument with Casey weighed heavily on Ridge as he shook the snow off and made his way to the waiting room of the hospital. Finding all his sons, he was relieved to hug Pike, who told him Sun and Paislee were stable, though not out of the woods.

"Still waiting for test results," Pike repeated for Ridge's sake.

"You look wrung out," Ridge said to his son, with concern in his voice.

"And you look like you need to be somewhere else," Pike told him before leaving again, in earshot of the family. Pike heard rumblings of his dad's date. This artist, often more sensitive to life's subtleties than the others, picked up on the sadness, too.

Ridge nodded in agreement.

"We had words."

"Go work things out," Pike said. "Go with my blessing—there's nothing you can do here, Dad. I appreciate your support, but I suspect someone else needs it just as much."

Sensing his family's approval, Ridge put his hat back on and buttoned his coat.

"Be safe, Dad, and stay in touch please," Gunnar said, "there's a full force blizzard coming down this way from the Pass."

"I'm sure she's right in town, at one of the houses," Ridge assured them, and left.

Just before reaching the sliding doors, Ridge heard Ash calling him. The boy was jogging through the lobby with his phone in his hand.

"I heard from Amber," Ash said urgently. "Casey drove up to the Pass—to try and get the Barber Ranch listing. She left half an hour ago, and Amber hasn't heard from her since."

Ridge sighed deeply and shook his head.

"I was afraid of that."

"You're going after her. Let me come with you."

Ridge took a full look at his youngest son who now towered over him, with a heart as big as all outdoors. Ridge was so proud, but had to do this alone.

"I'll make quick work of this—I can be at that ranch and back before the sun goes down. I'll stop home and get emergency gear, and a snow machine to tow. You stay here and keep us in your prayers. Start looking at colleges for us to visit this spring, okay?"

Ash looked worried, but nodded as Ridge turned to follow Casey. The sky was gray, and already darkening. The gust of frigid wind that hit Ash when the sliders opened was no joke, and held a taste of the ominous conditions heading towards the town like a speeding train.

Snow was already blanketing the Pass, Ash knew.

"TURN RIGHT ON 'AR 'ER RO'..."

Casey wondered what she ever did without a GPS telling her where to go—especially on Wyoming back roads, with snow coming down. But her reception and directions were breaking up as she got further from town. She knew enough to turn onto Barber Road, and that should take her right to the ranch.

She should not have ventured out in this weather, but it was too early in the season for the big snows, wasn't it? That's what she thought when she left for Barber Ranch. Today's rumor had it that the first agent to put a lock box on the front door could have the listing, and the commission on this heritage property would be substantial.

"I've got to take care of myself," Casey said out loud as she drove to bolster her courage. The conversation she had earlier with Ridge was upsetting, to say the least, and she had to get out of her apartment.

For a few sweet days, she had been so happy, falling in love with the cowboy she'd been dreaming of for so long. His kisses, his smiles and his touch were everything she hoped they would be. Ridge was loving and attentive, playful and sincere.

He was too good.

Casey couldn't drag his good name down with her own. She wasn't directly to blame for what happened in Phoenix, but she couldn't go to every single resident in West Gorge and explain her side of the story.

Facts were facts. Her father's company closed its doors, thanks to her, and employees weren't paid. Contracts were voided, and obligations weren't met. Sellers lost out on buyers; buyers lost out on properties. Jobs were lost.

Casey was lost!

"Oh no, this is bad." She'd been so lost in her thoughts she didn't notice how deep the snow was until her car was sinking and sliding into a drift, off to the side. She put the car in reverse and then forward, trying to rock it out of the ruts, but she was wedged tight.

Almost immediately, her engine stalled out. Casey sat in the quiet of the blizzard, listening only to the wind. Her windows were covered almost immediately with snow.

"What have I done?" She cried out, but nobody heard. Her car was dead, her phone had no reception, and Casey was nowhere near shelter.

CHAPTER 44

"Call Casey!"

In vain, Ridge shouted to his car speaker, which was already crackling and unresponsive on the remote road. He looked down at his phone briefly and pushed the button with her number on it, but she didn't answer.

Oh, Casey.

Ridge was making his way up the Pass in his four-wheel-drive, with wiper blades struggling to keep the snow off the windshield. He stopped at the ranch to hook up a towing trailer with a snowmobile on the back, for when his truck wouldn't go any further. He'd have to remember to thank the hands for keeping things in good working order at all times, so they were never caught unaware. It could mean the difference between life and death on a day like today.

Shaking his head in anger at her, Ridge knew that ambition blinded Casey to the dangers of the Wyoming elements, which she was still new to. But guilt also gnawed at Ridge's own stomach, wondering how big a role he played in driving her into the arms of sheer recklessness. He's the one who lit a competitive fire under her, and made her feel as though they were always in a race to the finish.

Ridge said a silent prayer for her safety, and his. People perished quickly in the Wyoming wilderness for silly reasons such as this—*a real estate listing.*

Sure, the commission would be hefty. And yes, her scumbag boyfriend from Phoenix was breathing down her neck for money. Ridge would help her sort out these problems, if only Casey would...

Whoa!

Ridge swerved on a patch of ice, nearly careening off the road and into a deep ditch.

"Pay attention," he yelled to himself while correcting the truck—the road to Barber Ranch was just ahead. Ridge recalled the last time he went to visit Chuck Barber before he passed away, a few years before. If he remembered right, there was nothing between the main road and the ranch, except maybe an abandoned one-room cabin.

It wasn't much, but it would keep Casey safe from the elements.

If she made it to the house, she'd have the sense to break in and hunker down until help could arrive. Ridge shook his head in anger at the numskull who said "first agent to put a lockbox on the front door can have the listing." Probably one of the idiot Barber boys, hoping to unload the ranch before winter and make a few dollars. Ridge was thankful for the sense his own sons have, due to their mother, no doubt.

But these details didn't matter now. The only thing that mattered was doing his best to find Casey Parks, because... *because...* And though the snow was heavy and blocked his view, he could clearly see his own motives for the first time.

He wanted to save his *wife*.

He couldn't stop the cancer years ago; couldn't save Randi Lynn, though he tried his best. And no one could stop this blizzard. But Casey was going to die in the snowstorm if he didn't find her, and he wasn't going to let his wife die again.

"Well I'll be, Lord," Ridge spoke in amazement and wonder to the icy windshield. "You really are giving me a second chance."

Turning carefully onto the ranch road, Ridge drove only a mile before finding his truck stuck in deep snow. He wondered how far Casey was able to get in her car.

Zzzz zzzz... the truck wheels spun and spit snow and ice as his car slid sideways. Not wanting it to get jammed in the embankment, Ridge put the truck in park with resignation. He zipped up his coat and pulled his hat over his ears. While at the ranch, he had put on warm snow pants and Arctic boots, and shoved below-zero gloves into his down parka.

He also grabbed a large backpack carrying a first aid kit, and stuffed it with supplies from the ranch shed—snow clothes for Casey, water bottles and granola bars and such, along with a flare gun, and a small pistol. People may not be out in the storm but hungry animals were, like wolves and coyotes.

The last thing Ridge did he hated to do, and that was turning off the engine and stepping out of the warm truck, into the cold wind and deep powder. Only the thought of Casey, cold, scared and alone could make him do this.

It was worse than he expected—the wind was strong, blowing icy snow into Ridge's exposed face. He pulled down the shield on the helmet, and started the snowmobile. If Casey was anywhere at all near the road, Ridge figured, she would hear him.

In spite of the snow and wind, Ridge could see the faintest indentation of tire tracks on the road which made him believe he was on the right track. Someone came up this road, he only hoped it was Casey, and not one of the Barber boys. He didn't want to waste his energy rescuing an idiot.

"Why didn't you turn around?" Ridge shouted out, though nobody could hear. It was enough to release the anger and frustration at their predicament, but there was plenty more of both bottled up inside him, he knows.

He wished she had returned to West Gorge while there was time to be safe. Or better yet, just stayed home in the first place. To be so driven to get a listing on a house that you would put your life in jeopardy was beyond Ridge, although a little part of him understood.

It was that same attitude of survival that his ancestors had when they were homesteading—they did what they had to do.

Casey would've made a good pioneer. She was bold and headstrong, just like another woman he knew when he was much younger. Maybe that's why he liked her so much. In the five years since Randi had died, Ridge never considered he might have a second chance at love until he met Casey. Now, he hoped he wasn't too late.

The snowmobile glided through the thick snow although none too quickly. Visibility was low with the heavy flakes coming down in the gray sky. Hopefully he would find Casey before full dark, which was only an hour away, at best.

Lord willing, if he found her, they'd have time to get to safety. Back to the truck, if they were lucky.

Ridge blew passed the abandon cabin, almost invisible in the heavy snow. He slowed, but didn't see any tracks near the door or any sign that Casey was there.

"OK, let's keep going," he said to himself, just to hear his own voice in the wilderness. When he was younger this would've been a great adventure. He loved being in Wyoming in the snow; the pines were so tall way up on the mountain tops. The gorge, which rarely froze, was covered with snow on the surrounding boulders and fallen logs.

Ridge never got tired of the view. But more and more he enjoyed viewing it from the picture window of the Lodge, next to the warmth of the roaring fire. With a hot coffee in his hand. This winter storm was a little more full-frontal than he'd experienced in a long time.

It was frigid and brutal and numbing, but he felt alive. He only hoped...

And then, after what felt like an hour, Ridge saw a flash of color ahead of him. He slowed down to see a little bit of red sticking out. It was Casey's car, fully buried in snow and sitting at an angle in a ditch.

Quickly, Ridge hopped off to wipe off the window.

There he saw Casey, slumped over the wheel. Not moving or responding.

CHAPTER 45

"Casey!"

Her door was locked, but a few hard pounds on the frame roused her. Shock and surprise registered on her face. *Ridge,* she mouthed, and scrambled to unlock the door.

As snow poured into the car with the wind, tears flowed down Casey's face as she fell against Ridge's open arms.

"I thought I was going to die out here alone."

"Come here baby, it's going to be okay," he said. "Let's get you home." Ridge hugged her as best he could while wearing the thick downy layers.

After a quick assessment of Casey's clothing, Ridge determined she needed more protection before they got back on the snowmobile. "Stay here," he said and trudged through the deep snow to get his backpack. He helped Casey slip a warmer anorak over her coat, and snow pants over her jeans.

He refrained from scolding or shaking his finger at her; there would be time for that. As it was, she could barely stop crying from fear, and the relief of being found.

The boots he brought were too big but had a thick flannel lining that would keep her feet warm. Like getting a five-year-old ready for

Kindergarten recess, he added a warm hat and gloves before stuffing her purse and keys in his backpack.

"Ready?"

I have promises to keep, and miles to go before I sleep.

A poem from school days came into Ridge's mind. He had only made promises to Casey in his heart, but he would surely keep them.

Casey hopped out of the car. The snow was so deep that she practically fell completely forward into Ridge, who caught her and helped her trudge to the snowmobile. Already covered in fresh snow, he swept off the seat and instructed her to hang onto his waist.

"It's slow going," he shouted through the wind. She merely nodded and buried her face in the back of his coat. He could feel her racking sobs as he worked to turn the snowmobile around. Ridge wanted to reassure Casey, but again, there would be plenty of time for that.

Cold, icy wind pounded him as he squinted to see this through the blizzard. The shield on his helmet was icing up as fast as he clumsily cleared it with his gloves. He was breathing hard, and wished he'd taken in some water when he stopped.

Rrrr rrrr... the snowmobile struggled with the deep powder and the weight of them both.

Finding a spot behind a line of trees, he stopped a few minutes in just to exhale and take a sip of water from a bottle in the side pocket of the backpack. He turned around and offered it to Casey. Her face was red and cold from the snow, and probably from crying. She looked miserable and scared. He probably looked the same.

With the motor shut off and the wind blocked, the air was quiet. The only sound was snowflakes falling off of thin branches. It was majestic on one hand, and terrifying on another. People perished in the mountains of Wyoming every year.

Hikers froze to death.

Fly fishers got swept away by flash floods in the rivers.

Mountain climbers lost their footing on ice.

And then...

"*Ridge,*" Casey called his name in fear—he held his hand up for silence.

Through the hat and helmet, Ridge could hear the growling of predators and his blood curdled. Coyotes, maybe wolves, were tracking them. With just one snowmobile, the hungry animals felt emboldened.

Ridge knew he just had to get them to the abandon cabin.

"Ridge?" Casey cried out, gripping him so tight that it mirrored the fear he felt in his own gut. He took a free hand and patted hers.

"There's an empty cabin up ahead," he said, turning the key in the ignition.

Pray we reach it in time.

The West Ranch has several outbuildings and barns with old cars, rusty tractors, and snowmobiles from years gone by—some that could be museum pieces, even. And maybe he should donate them to the town historical society. Ridge was glad he'd taken the newest snow-mobile on this journey, making sure the tank was full of gas.

With a quiet determination, Ridge made his way through the deep snow with Casey on the back. The snow came down hard, and it was getting dark. He didn't want to miss the cabin again. Eventually, through the inky woods, he saw it on his left and nearly sobbed in relief.

He was riding like a pack of wolves was on his tail, which was probably true.

At the cabin, he parked the machine under a half-fallen lean-to by a side wall, then used a flashlight to locate several large branches and evergreen boughs to cover it as best he could—if the doorway was wider, he'd bring it inside.

Casey tried to help, but kept falling in the deep snow. He was spending too much time helping her stand again and again.

"Get the backpack," he yelled through the wind.

At last, taking her arm, they found the door which was half buried in snow. Thankfully, it pushed inward and one strong kick was all the old wood needed.

Inside was pitch dark and just as cold as outside, minus the wind.

The windows were cracked but not quite broken. Nobody had been there in years, from the looks of it. There was rudimentary wooden furniture, if you could call the pieces that, and a few ancient logs near the stone fireplace.

"Here we are," he said, pulling a small emergency lantern from the backpack and turning it on. Ridge shined his flashlight inside the stone fireplace and could see flecks of light. A good sign. He could try to make a fire without the smoke choking them back outside.

Ridge found a lighter and a fire starter which he set on the ancient logs. They would burn quickly he knew, and looked around. He'd have no choice but to burn the few sticks of furniture, and whatever else he could get his hands on. Their survival depended on it.

Sitting on the floor near the fireplace, coaxing the flames, Ridge could hear wolves too close to the cabin. Their howls chilled his blood, and he knew Casey must be frightened out of her mind. But he'd have to put on his bravest smile and calm her fears.

"Do you hear them?" Casey asked him nervously, her voice shaking.

Of course he did—the howls practically drowned out her words.

"Hear what?" Ridge said, and in spite of themselves, and the seriousness of their predicament, Casey joined him on the floor and they laughed until they cried.

CHAPTER 46

A small fire burning in the fireplace took the chill off, and made everything feel hopeful again. Ridge scavenged anything he could find in the little room to keep it burning. There was a broken chair and he easily snapped the legs off of the rotting wood. The little wooden table would be next, followed by another broken chair and some assorted wood Ridge could not even make out.

As the flames warmed the room, Ridge took a quick inventory of his backup fuel supply—rotted floor boards, the trim around the windows, and a loose rafter. Whatever it would take to keep Casey warm, and wolves at bay.

The door was tightly latched, and it didn't take long for Casey and Ridge to breathe a sigh of relief and remove some of their heavy outer layers to hang on pegs along the wall.

Together, they sat with their backs against the log wall gazing at the fire.

"I can't believe you came to find me," Casey said. "I didn't think anybody would come looking for me. Thank you."

Ridge could only nod, and maybe he should have kept his mouth shut. But he couldn't.

"Why did you run up here in a storm—just for an idiotic *listing*?"

"You… your family… it was a lot. I don't belong."

"You're going to have to get over that," Ridge said. "I'm a package deal. But I promise you, nobody bites."

"I guess I thought I'd be compared to… Randi."

Ridge looked closely, and saw just how fragile even the toughest of women could be.

"I've never compared you," he said, simply. "I see you, Casey Parks. I see who you are."

Casey leaned her head against him, and Ridge pulled her close as he closed his eyes.

"Randi's time came and went, and she left her mark on me. A beautiful, lovely mark. I can never forget the time we had and I don't want to. You wouldn't want me to. That's not the kind of man you want— the kind that can forget a woman so easily."

The kind of man you had, Ridge thought.

"But here and now, this is our time," he said, sleepily.

As Ridge closed his eyes, his thoughts swirled from the exertion and emotion of the day. Waking just a few hours later, he felt despair at seeing the diminishing flames. He tried to untangle from Casey, but they both woke up.

"Time to get some more furniture on this fire. I don't know who owns this cabin, but I'm sure I'm going to have to buy it from them, or at least buy them some new furniture. I'll leave him a note before we go."

"Maybe it's for sale," Casey said, perhaps trying to lighten the mood.

"Maybe you wanna beat me to the listing, and put both our lives in danger again." Ridge knew his words sounded harsh, but he felt scared. He didn't know how long he'd be able to protect Casey or himself, and he had a lot to live for.

Three of his four sons were newly married, and his first grandchild was growing up right under his roof. He had a teenage boy he vowed to protect like a father should, and yet he put himself at risk. Because *she* put herself at risk.

Casey began crying again.

"I'm sorry," she said. "It never occurred to me that you would rescue me. I thought I'd have to live and die by my own decisions."

"There's more dying than living with that philosophy, Casey."

"It's works well enough," she said, "until you come to the end of yourself, and realize there's no one else."

Ridge nodded.

"We're all guilty of that I suppose," he said, then rooted around the backpack and pulled out a few apples and granola bars.

"Dinner is served," he said with a smile.

Casey smiled back.

"I brought a bottle of chilled Riesling," he said, handing her a bottle of the water.

"Oh, that's a good year," she joked back. Ridge was glad to see her smiling again.

"So," he looked around the room, "if this was for sale, what would your vision be—what would you do with the kitchen?"

"Add one," she said with a weak laugh.

Ridge wanted to laugh, until he heard howling outside reminding him there were wolves waiting outside his door. He stoked the fire with the little table and one of the other chairs. There wasn't a lot of furniture left, hopefully they could make do until daylight.

He would keep the gun handy, maybe put it in the pocket of his parka before they left in the morning. He didn't know how long he could keep the pack away, but he would try his best. Casey was nervous, he could tell.

"The décor is nice." Ridge looked around at the objects on the wall from a bygone era. There were a couple snow shoes laced with elk sinew, and a handsaw with teeth that had been worn down and rusted, no doubt from being left outside in the rain for years. An oval frame held a picture of a man and a woman who looked like they could be his great grandparents, Pickford and Addie West.

Ridge settled back again against the wall, and motioned with his free arm for Casey to do the same. She nestled against him as if it were the most natural thing in the world, and he hugged her tight. She was flesh and blood, bone and spirit, and his earlier feelings were confirmed—he had fallen deeply in love with her.

"Why did you come searching for me Ridge?" Casey asked, as if sensing his thoughts.

"Because you don't have people in your life, only cold empty houses."

"Lots of people fall into that category Ridge. Why did you come searching for *me*?"

"You make me feel needed, and I've been without that feeling for a long time."

"Ash needs you. Your family needs you," she said.

Ridge frowned in the darkened room—Casey wasn't letting him off hook. He didn't like being pushed into speaking words he'd only started thinking. At last, Ridge sighed and gave in. There was something about the situation and the dark cabin that loosened him.

"The *need* I'm talking about is sacred, Casey; that place where a man and woman join in body, spirit and soul. I thought that was behind me—until I met you. You make me crazy. I can't understand half of the things you do. But I need you."

"Oh," Casey said simply as she lifted her head to see his face.

In the glow of the fire, she liked what she saw—silvery stubble on his chin, the wild hair of an adventurer, and eyes that were like clear blue arrows, aimed directly at her. And now, he was showing her his heart.

He lifted his hand on her back and moved it slowly around and down, exploring the feel of her curves. "You're like a... *kitten*," he said, "that won't stop climbing trees. And I want to be the man who rescues you."

She moved closer.

"I thought I told you..." she said in a whisper, moving her hand up to caress the soft stubble on his jaw, "I don't need rescuing."

The corner of his mouth lifted in half a smile.

"Did it occur to you that I might?"

She opened her lips in surprise, but no words could escape. Ridge pulled her to himself and gently covered her mouth with his own. He kissed her for a long time as they leaned into each other.

"Oh my..." Casey gasped as she pulled away, but then brought her mouth to his once again. He tasted warm and alive. And with each kiss, her body started coming to life, in a way she'd never known. Certainly not with... no, she wouldn't even think his name while Ridge West was kissing and holding her.

CHAPTER 47

*R*idge was astounded with each of Casey's kisses.
He stepped through a door he'd been afraid to open since Randi died, and it was like stepping into Oz—there was still color to be had in his life, not just the black-and-white scenarios of his recent existence.

He was alive, and suddenly wide awake.

"Casey..." he whispered into her ear, and she moaned in response.

He didn't know what words he meant to say, but had to say her name. Finally, he made himself pull away from her kiss, to catch his breath. But he nuzzled his face into her hair, and waited for his breathing to slow down. She was doing the same, he could tell.

Ridge sit back against the wall and held her. Eventually, they fell asleep. A few hours later, they woke to the anemic sun peeking through the trees.

"Wind has died down some, but it's still snowing. We'd better head out." Ridge said to Casey, who nodded through a frown.

"Hey," he said, standing up and offering his hand, "thank you."

He reached down and caressed her cheek.

"For what?" she asked.

"For last night."

Casey gave a soft laugh. "No comment. But I should be thanking you again for rescuing me. If you hadn't, I'd be freezing to death in my car."

"We're not out of the woods yet," he said, with that low rumble in his voice that she loved. "Let's get out of here, and see if we can get to my truck; it's close to the main road. Hopefully the plows are out."

"Do you think... before we go?"

"What?" he asked, feeling impatient. The fire was dying, and it was getting cold in the cabin.

"One more kiss? I want to be sure I wasn't just dreaming last night."

Ridge smiled, and she adored the way his eyes crinkled.

He leaned in, only this time he kissed her on her cheeks, softly and tenderly. She hummed in delight, and drank in the sensation.

GETTING the snowmobile out and into the snow was much harder than parking it had been. Several more inches fell in the night and the powder was a formidable enemy. Casey pushed from behind while Ridge pulled on the handlebars. The snowmobile was their best chance for surviving.

Before they left the cabin, Ridge scribbled a note of apology and stuck it on a nail jutting out from the mantle. At the last minute, he yanked the ancient snow shoes off the wall and strapped them to the backpack.

"Just in case," he said to Casey.

He also slipped the pistol out of the pack and into his parka, making sure the safety latch was secured. He put the flare gun where he could reach it quickly. He had a few encounters with wolves over the years, but had been able to warn them off. The deep snow made them vulnerable, though, and the snowmobile would be sluggish.

They were about to get on the snowmobile, when Ridge saw movement out of the corner of his eye, deep into the woods. She must have seen it too.

He turned around and took Casey in his arms one more time. "I'm going to do my best to get us home," he said. "And then I want to have a long talk with you about what that means for the two of us."

Casey hugged him hard and got on the back.

The snowmobile started up quickly, but the road itself was nowhere to be found. It was just a space between the tree line, with snow so deep that it would be a miracle to not get caught in a drift.

Making their way, Ridge saw movement again. He was struggling just to see what was ahead of him, and didn't want to stop. He took a quick glance, and saw a flash of what could be fur and teeth and eyes —but maybe that was his imagination.

He heard a growl.

There was a time when wolves were afraid of snowmobiles, but many had become accustomed to people and small vehicles. And fearless with their hunger.

After too short a while, the snowmobile slowed in a snow drift and then stopped.

"*No, no,*" Ridge exclaimed. He turned the key in the ignition a couple of times, but nothing happened. He'd pushed it too hard. The engine was flooded from his efforts.

"What now?" Casey called out, with fear in her voice.

"Now we go on foot," Ridge said, trying to muster as much confidence as his voice as possible. "We will use the snow shoes," he said.

The old sinew snow shoes were brittle, but designed to last. Using some rope from his backpack, he lashed first one and then another around the front of Casey's boots. The pair he wore still had its leather intact, so hopefully they would stay on top of the deep powder so they could make headway.

"Ridge," Casey cried out, spotting a wolf behind the trees. He knew they were extremely vulnerable. He pulled out the pistol and turned, firing a warning shot above their heads.

CHAPTER 48

"Someone wanted to come down from the pediatric ward to see you," Pike said, walking into the hospital room where Paislee rested—as much as she could rest with constant activity from doctors and nurses.

"She was a little dehydrated from an ear infection—quite common in babies, they tell me—and she's doing fine," Pike said. "If her fever is down, she'll come home tomorrow, when you do."

Paislee opened her eyes to see Sun curled up on Pike's chest like a little ball, and thought her heart would explode with happiness at the sight. The baby turned towards Paislee and smiled through flushed cheeks.

"Hello you," Paislee cooed.

"Sun wanted me to tell you that she's heard from our attorneys," Pike went on. "They have spoken with all parties, and filed papers so we can adopt her. It will take a while, but they do not expect anyone to contest this. The grandmother won't, or the Chens. The adoption of Sun into the West family has officially taken on a life of its own."

While Pike said this, Paislee saw how he absentmindedly kissed the top of the baby's head, and snuggled her close. As if it were the most natural thing in the world.

"Something else has taken on a life of its own," Paislee said softly, pulling an envelope from her nightstand and handing it to her husband. "I'll trade you."

As she took Sun in her arms, careful to maneuver around her IV drip and blood pressure cuff, Pike opened the folded paper and a photo negative floated to the floor like a leaf falling off a tree. Picking it up, he could see cone-shaped rays surrounding the cloudy images of...

"We are pregnant, you and me," she said with an incredulous laugh.

Pike's mouth dropped open, and he reached behind for a chair to fall into.

"Sun is going to be a big sister in the summer."

His eyes could not get any bigger, nor his mouth any wider at his shock. When he recovered enough to trust his legs, he moved to sit on the edge of the bed and put both arms around his wife and baby—*both babies!*

Tears welled up in Pike's eyes, but no words came to his lips.

"Kat said this sometimes happens—when a mother has a baby in her arms, her body relaxes about becoming pregnant, and it's not such a big deal," Paislee said.

"But it is a big deal," Pike said, soberly. "I'm sorry for not realizing how big a deal this is... for you, and for us."

Paislee shook her head.

"I had no idea either, Pike," she said. "Not until I married you, and my happiness just seemed to burst like fireworks on the fourth of July—then I knew how badly I wanted a family with you. I'm the one who's sorry for making this such a big deal, and being so preoccupied. We had all the time in the world, I guess. I suppose I simply wanted to know that we *could.*"

"Oh we can, and we did," Pike said, taking the baby gently from Paislee.

"Say goodbye to Mama," he crooned to Sun, "I promised the nurses we'd only be gone for a few minutes."

Mama.

Paislee's tears raced her smile to see which would be first. It was a tie.

She secretly feared Pike might suggest *returning* Sun, now that a baby of their own was on the way. Just the thought caused her anxiety, but she should have known better.

CHAPTER 49

*E*ven in the wind, Ridge could hear the alpha wolf whimper in surprise and fear as he led his pack to retreat into the trees. If each shot bought a little time, it might add up to safety.

"Let's go," he said, taking Casey's hand and pulling her at a faster pace than she was ready for. By his calculations, they had another hour on foot before reaching his car. Ridge felt more than saw the wolves tracking them again, and tried to calculate the few bullets left in the pistol. He should have brought more.

Hearing a growl that was a lot closer than any of the previous growls, Ridge motioned to Casey to stop and step behind him. He took his glove off and tried grip the gun, but his bare hand was cold and stiff. Before he could stop it, the gun fell into the deep snow, just as a gust of wind blinded Ridge, and covered all traces of the hole.

He reached down to retrieve it but it was lost.

"Ridge, they're getting closer," Casey cried out.

"Quick, turn around so I can get the flare gun."

Casey pivoted so he could pull the flare gun from pack. She felt a scream well up in her throat that she tried to swallow—it felt as though the wolves were circling them.

Ridge lifted his arm above their heads and fired the flare gun, partially into the trees and partially into the sky. The heavy snow muffled the sound, but amplified the flares. The wolves whimpered once again and ran, hopefully for longer than the last time.

"Fast as you can," Ridge said again, grabbing Casey's hand.

Tramping through the drifts, he could feel her becoming paralyzed by fear. They were both discouraged by their lack of progress, but it was up to him to stay positive and lead her.

If the wolves wanted to attack, Ridge knew, there was very little he could do to fend them off. They walked for another 15 minutes or so, before sensing the wolves getting near once again. Without the pistol or the flare gun, they were helpless. Their only hope was to reach the car in time and Ridge doubted they would.

"Did I ever tell you Casey," Ridge said in a loud but conversational voice, "when I first fell in love with you?"

Casey jerked and froze at his words, but he gave her hand a firm tug.

"Keep walking. It was when I saw you talking to Ash and being so generous with your advice. And I was being an ass," he said, "yet you took it like a champ. I was thoroughly ashamed of myself and so impressed with you at the same time."

"Ridge..." Casey sounded like she was going to scream at the wolves nearby, but then exhaled and kept walking.

"Once we get home," Ridge turned to look her in the eye with all the bravado he could muster, "once we get *home*, I'm going to give Ash my little house on Madison, and leave you two vultures to the real estate business."

Casey squeezed his hand and smiled. As if they weren't about to topple over from exhaustion; as if they weren't about to be attacked by ravenous wolves.

"Did I ever tell you when I started falling in love with you?" Casey yelled so Ridge could hear her in the storm. "I was sitting next to you in that jail cell, and you were so cute the way you thought neither of us had won that little house. The look on your face when I told you that my assistant made the bid for me, well it just broke my heart."

"I didn't think you had a heart," Ridge shouted into the snow.

"I guess I did, and I guess you just about stole it, and broke it, then stole it again."

"I love you Casey Parks, will you be my wife?"

Ridge felt her slow down again.

"Keep going," he shouted. "I'd get down on my knee, but it hurts. And I'd sink to Colorado in this deep powder. But I'll ask you properly when I can. Don't slow down."

Don't slow down.

She was crying, he could tell, whether from love or fright he did not know or care. He would be there for her until the end, no matter when.

Every instinct told Ridge that the wolves we're going to make a move, and a voice in his head, probably an old scouting leader, said to stop and find a weapon. He could pull a few branches off of a tree, one for him and one for Casey, but he knew that would only buy them seconds.

He felt like crying at the hopelessness he felt. He wanted so badly to save Casey, just as she had saved him. But the car—and safety—was nowhere in sight.

"Casey…" he started to say, wanting to give her final words of love; words that might be the last he ever said, before he covered her body with his own, in a final act of desperate courage. But before he could form a sentence, he heard another sound; another growl in the distance was getting close, fast.

A grizzly?

No, it couldn't be. Though it sounded like a pack of grizzlies.

Squinting in confusion, Ridge saw lights bouncing off of the trees, and had hope for the first time that day. The wolves practically grazed Ridge's legs as they yelped and darted into the woods before another pack overtook them—huge snowmobiles charging through the drifts and stopping in front of the stunned pair.

CHAPTER 50

"*D*ad!"

It was Gunnar, Colton, and two men from the West Gorge search and rescue team. Ridge wanted to cry and kiss them all. He let out a sob in relief that Casey would be safe.

"We saw your flare and turned towards it," Colton said with obvious emotion and relief in his voice. "Good job, Dad."

Ridge tried to speak, but could only pull Casey into a clumsy embrace as he kissed the side of her hat. He got a mouth full of snow but didn't care.

Trembling and spent, Ridge allowed his sons to help them take their next steps.

"Let's get you guys home to West Gorge," one search and rescue man said. "You've been exposed to a lot of elements. I've radioed the hospital, and they are expecting you."

Ridge knew better than to argue, especially with Dr. Kat calling the shots, as he suspected she was. He helped Casey onto the back of one of the rescue snowmobiles.

"Thank God for all of you," Ridge manage to say before getting on the other rescue snowmobile. Ridge did his best to embrace Gunnar and Colton, but whatever strength he might have felt moments ago, left him completely.

As the machines turned around to make their way to the main road, Ridge looked over at the future Mrs. West, with a heart full of love and gratitude.

RIDING on the back of the rescue snowmobile, Casey Parks cried freely until she was spent. Nobody could hear her over the engines, she knew, and her driver was too busy navigating the drifts to worry about her emotional well-being.

That will be her husband's job.

Looking over, she could see Ridge on the back of the other rescue rider's snowmobile, with his sons flanking them on either side. Casey never felt so safe or secure in her entire life—not since childhood.

She looked forward to meeting Ridge's family properly, and thanking his sons for coming out in a blizzard to find them. Of course, she knew they came to rescue Ridge—but Ridge... now that was another matter altogether. Ridge came to rescue *her*. He saved her life. And then asked her to marry him.

Did she accept?

Casey couldn't remember, but would say yes just as soon as they got to the hospital. Before he tried to give her a "better" proposal than the one she got today. It was perfect.

It was *sacred.*

CHAPTER 51

TWO MONTHS LATER

"*L*et me see that ring one more time," Pepper Andrews asked Casey, now Casey West, as they sat down in Paislee's farmhouse. "I heard he made you sign a *pre-nup*."

"Mama!" Paislee laughed at her mother from the kitchen.

"Well, is it true?" Pepper ignored her daughter. She and Casey each sat with a small plate of mini spring rolls, and cherry tomatoes cut into tiny tuna cups. Behind them was a tall Christmas tree, and a banner that read: It's A Boy!

Paislee's parents, sisters, and grandmother came to West Gorge to spend Christmas. It was the perfect time for a baby shower, Kat and Liu thought, especially since the weather had been mild, and roads were navigable.

As a few dozen women milled around the baby shower and laughed in groups, these two sat together on a loveseat, enjoying the fireplace in relative peace.

"Yes, I did sign a pre-nuptial agreement before we got married," Casey confessed. "Ridge made me promise that, as his wife, I would never climb a tree, break into an abandoned house, or drive into a blizzard for the sake of a listing. 'Til death do us part."

"That is the most romantic thing I've ever heard," Pepper practically swooned.

Casey laughed along with her.

Becoming fast friends, Ridge and Casey planned to meet Pepper and Drake Andrews for a cruise and tour of Italy and Greece in the spring, after a honeymoon in the Swiss Alps. They'd return in time for Gunnar and Kat to take a long overdue vacation with Willow.

Everyone wanted to be back for the arrival of Mr. Ford West, due to Pike and Paislee in the summer. They were all over the moon excited.

"Where are you going to live?" Pepper wanted to know next.

"That is a good question," Casey replied.

"Next door to us," Paislee and Liu said simultaneously.

"Now wait a minute," Kat objected. "I'm hoping they'll stay at the ranch."

"You're all too kind," Casey said, truly touched. But she and Ridge had a lot of options. They could build on the ranch, or in Colton's new development. They might find a house in town. Small enough for two of them, with room for Ash when he wanted to join them. And large enough to host family dinners every now and then.

"I'd really like Bud Shire's house," Ridge often teased his wife. "If only I knew a realtor who could get it for me."

As for Casey, she just didn't care where they lived. Her apartment, the ranch, and the Madison house all took turns. They even spent a few days in Casey's family home in Phoenix, where they decided to end their renters' contract and have the house completely renovated. After all, they'd need a place to stay to meet with their attorney, and for court hearings.

Ridge convinced Casey to file charges against Derek Vance for embezzlement and extortion. It was the only way, he said, to truly have peace, and closure.

And hold that old dog accountable, Ridge thought to himself.

"You didn't have had friends, resources, or *fight* in you when he did this—but we have them all, now," he told his bride. That was just before introducing her to Randi's friend in Arizona, the judge they'd visited years ago, who had no hesitation issuing a search warrant for Derek's bank records and phone conversations.

When the dust settled, they agreed the house in Phoenix would make a nice winter retreat, away from the Wyoming blizzards—which neither had an affinity for. The Parks house was perfectly situated near restaurants, galleries, and coffee shops.

Yes, the new Mr. and Mrs. West certainly had options, Casey knew. But wherever she woke up next to Ridge, with his salt and pepper whiskers, and gravelly morning voice calling her name—that was Casey's home.

END

* * *

Ready for more of The Wild Wests romance series? Read *Her Unexpected Cowboy* free, then get ready for Ash's love story in *Sassy Cowgirl Kisses*, now available for pre-order.

HER UNEXPECTED COWBOY, A FREE STORY IN THE WILD WESTS ROMANCE SERIES

She was looking for a cowboy, not a nerd. Then a dangerous bull moose reveals a cowboy heart beating in the chest of this city slicker.

JAYCEE'S AUNT thinks she should broaden her horizons beyond the dusty cowboys she normally dates. But her aunt's latest set-up with Josh, a nerdy city-boy doctor, is way outside her comfort zone. He's nothing like the rough and tumble men she's normally attracted to... until they have a run-in with a rogue moose, and Josh shows Jaycee that being a true cowboy is about a lot more than wearing pointy boots and a hat.

CLICK HERE to download your free story, or go to KathyFawcett.com

ARE YOU READY FOR MORE SWEET ROMANCE? GET READY FOR ASH'S LOVE STORY IN *SASSY COWGIRL KISSES*, NUMBER 5 IN THE WILD WESTS ROMANCE SERIES, NOW AVAILABLE FOR PRE-ORDER ON AMAZON.COM

Ash West returns to West Ranch after college and falls for Sassy, the new ranch hand. She's outspoken, bold and beautiful, and hides a secret that will rock the West's tranquil Wyoming life.

OTHER BOOKS BY KATHY FAWCETT

Her Quarantined Cowboy
Wild Wests #1

Their blind date is a disaster, and both are happy when it's cut short. Then a quick spreading virus forces Kat to lock down the hospital—with Gunnar inside. He hates being stuck anywhere, with anyone. But Dr. Kat is the new sheriff in town, and she won't let him bend the rules in her hospital. Forced to work together, anger turns to admiration--which turns to romance. But can it last when the quarantine is over?

Drawing Her Cowboy
Wild Wests #2

Beautiful and rich, Paislee seems to have a perfect life – but she feels like she's losing herself in the smothering grip of her controlling fiancée. So when her grandmother suggests a road trip to unravel a family mystery, she jumps at the chance. She is determined to find answers, and finds more than she bargained for when she follows Pike to the old settler's barn. Trapped by a blizzard, Paislee is soon wearing a prairie dress and dining by candlelight with the cowboy who caught her imagination. Will he catch her heart, too?

Stirring Her Cowboy
Wild Wests #3

Life is fun and games for Colton West, until his steamy introduction to ranch's beautiful new cook. But she's a trained chef, not some chuckwagon bean-slinger, and wants Colton to simmer down. When their grizzled old camp cook retires, the last thing Colton expects is to fall in love with his replacement. But when Chef Liu Chen feeds his body and soul, his heart isn't far behind.

Liu is an accomplished and confident fourth-generation Chinese-American. Her family lineage of Wyoming ancestors is as thick and rich as her bechamel sauce. Remembering the struggles and heartbreaks of their ancestors, her parents and grandparents discourage her from falling in love with a cowboy. But Colton is not going down without a fight. And Liu's heart begins to soften toward this man working so hard to earn her love.

Shoulder Season

Lake Michigan Lodge #1

Kay is finally renovating her lodge and her life. Now who will she share it with? In this funny uplifting tale of renovation, redemption and romance, a rustic old lodge on Lake Michigan isn't the only thing that gets a second chance.

Water Dance

Lake Michigan Lodge #2

In Book #2 of the Lake Michigan Lodge Series, can Kay's happy-ever-after survive an invasion of teenage girls?

ABOUT THE LAKE MICHIGAN LODGE SERIES

A rambling vintage tourist lodge nestled in a sunny bay on Lake Michigan is the only home wise-cracking Kay Kerby has ever known. She loves Kerby Lodge. But running it? Not so much. As far as Kay is concerned, the best season begins when the last lodger packs up their sunscreen and novelty t-shirts and goes home. Now an epic snowstorm pounds the coastline, and a blizzard of bills and taxes threaten to bury Kerby Lodge.

But the storms Kay doesn't see coming are the unpredictable Mayne brothers —a cloud of curls and attitude named Daniel and his younger brother Luke, a nomadic school teacher. After a devastating career loss, the mysterious Daniel just wants to be left alone. Kay is only too happy to oblige him. Then a freak accident and record-breaking blizzard leave them holed up together. Now the only person Kay can confide in is Luke, and he's thousands of miles away. Forced by walls of snow to face their broken dreams, Kay and Daniel set out on a journey of reclamation. In the process Kay finds herself hopelessly entangled with the Mayne brothers. One brother makes her laugh. The other just makes her crazy.

ABOUT THE AUTHOR

Kathy Fawcett is the author of sweet romantic comedy and women's fiction that will keep you smiling, crying and turning pages long past your bedtime. Kathy's funny dialogue and heartfelt stories make her a favorite with a growing number of fans.

Kathy transports readers to the surf, sand and snow of charming Lake Michigan towns, as well as the windswept mountains of Wyoming. Home is Michigan, where Kathy worked for years as an advertising writer. She met and married her husband Steve while students at Northern Michigan University, and he introduced her to his home state of Wyoming. Together, they reside near the Great Lakes with their bossy cat Sam, and are surrounded by grown children, growing grandchildren, and towering pine trees. Stay in touch with Kathy's latest books and projects by signing up for her newsletter (and get a free copy of *Her Unexpected Cowboy!*) reading her blog at kathyfawcett.com or emailing her at kathy@kathyfawcett.com

www.ingramcontent.com/pod-product-compliance
Lightning Source LLC
Chambersburg PA
CBHW05074223O626
17052CD00004BA/993